Aurora Isiana

by *Valeriya Salt*

abuddhapress@yahoo.com

ISBN: 9798373101127

Alien Buddha Press 2023

©™®

Valeriya Salt 2023

The following is a work of fiction. Any similarities to actual people, places, or events, unless deliberately expressed otherwise by the author are purely coincidental.

London, United Kingdom

2016

"I don't understand." Andrea shifted her gaze from the thick envelope to the lawyer and back. Her hands were shaking. "How is it possible? My mother never told me about you. In fact, my mother hasn't said a word to me for as long as I remember her. You know her mental condition—"

"Miss Zissman, I understand your shock and confusion." Mr Abram's pale eyes stared at her without a blink. "It must be hard for you to know that your mother died without saying her last goodbye or seeing you, but let me assure you that Mrs Zissman always tried to protect you and your interests."

"Protect me? From what? What are you talking about?" Andrea yelled. "My mum spent over thirty years in a special care home. She never recognised me or anybody else. My grandmother brought me up alone. Now, you're telling me that my mother talked to you but not to her family?"

"Miss Zissman, I am your mother's solicitor, not her doctor." The lawyer pursed his lips. "I've invited you to my office, following the last instructions of my deceased client. That's what I'm getting paid for. I have no intention to intervene in your family's relationships."

Andrea covered her face with her hands, trying to hide her tears. "I didn't visit Mother very often at her care home. That's true. Perhaps I wasn't a good daughter but... Why? Why did she never...?" Her last words drowned in sobs.

"Please, drink some water." Mr Abrams rose from his heavy wooden desk and went to the mini-bar.

He poured water from a jar and put it in front of Andrea. "I do apologise for my harsh tone, but you need to understand that my job is to protect the interests of my client. Not her family, friends, or any other entities."

Andrea kept silent. The letter she received a couple of days ago from Mr Abrams had taken her by surprise. At first, she thought it must've been just a standard procedure of reading the will, but it turned out there was much more to it. Her mother had a solicitor?

"Did you know my father?" she asked after a prolonged pause.

Mr Abrams sighed and turned to the wide window, clearly avoiding Andrea's gaze. "Only briefly. I'd met him once, a few weeks before his tragic death."

"And my grandmother? Did she instruct you to keep silent about my mother?"

"I had nothing to do with her or any other members of your family." Mr Abrams turned away from the window and returned to his desk.

Other members? I don't have any relatives left. Andrea frowned.

"Here is something else for you." He opened the top drawer and pulled out another, much smaller, white envelope.

Andrea opened it. "A key and a code?"

"A key for a deposit box." Mr Abrams nodded.

"Something so important that my mother didn't trust it even to her solicitor?" Andrea smirked, but the man didn't react to her taunt.

"Once again, I want to express my sincere condolences, Miss Zissman." He stretched his hand for a handshake, showing that her appointment was over. "My colleagues and I are always happy to help you with any legal issues."

Andrea scrambled to gather her belongings and, after a cold, formal goodbye, left the solicitor's office.

***

Andrea sat in the darkness of her car, trying to digest what had just happened.

It was late November, but there was almost no snow. Most of the shops, cafés, restaurants, and businesses tried to create a joyful atmosphere, decorating their windows, facades, and porches with traditional Christmas themes.

Andrea caught herself remembering that this was her mum's favourite time of the year. Tears started to burn her eyes again as she recalled her mother's smiling face every time she watched the illumination. *Why, Mother? Why?* She wiped her eyes with a handkerchief, switched on the light, and opened the thick envelope.

An old, faded photo from the seventies or eighties fell on her knees. The first one depicted her mother in a long, colourful dress and a huge, broad-brimmed hat, enjoying the summer somewhere on a sunny beach of the south coast. The sea breeze was blowing her red hair around, and she smiled happily… so young, full of energy and life. The photo had been taken long before her illness, long before Andrea was born.

She also found an old notepad, full of sketches. A lonely, flat peak of a mountain, a figure on skis, her father's portrait, a few seascapes - the same motives repeated again and again. Andrea must admit her mother was quite good at drawing. One attracted Andrea's attention: an eagle with spread wings. The symbol used by Nazi Germany. She frowned. The eagle was so random and out of place here. She turned the page and recognised her mother's sloppy writing

"Gabi," she read aloud.

The name was repeated a few more times. There were some more notes, but Andrea struggled to read them. The dim light of the car, the old paper, and the faded ink didn't help the matter.

She heard bells toll from a church nearby and shot a look at her watch. Five o'clock. She still had some time to go to the bank to check the deposit box.

To her luck, there were not many clients at such a late hour, and a clerk accompanied her to the vault straight away. The clerk explained the rules and left her alone. She inputted the code, turned the key, and opened the box with shaking hands. Her heart was pounding in her chest as peered inside.

"What the hell?" she yelled, fumbling in the empty deposit box. "Is it a joke? Are you kidding me?"

She picked up the phone on the wall and dialled the number that the clerk gave her.

A few minutes later, the same middle-aged woman appeared in the vault.

"The box is empty," Andrea blurted out. "How is it possible?"

"Well, it's possible that another key holder—" the clerk started with a polite fake smile.

"Another key holder? Who are they?"

"Unfortunately, the bank can't disclose their identity."

"This box belongs to my mother. She gave me a key and the code."

The lady shrugged. "Maybe it's worth asking your mother who else has access to the box."

"My mother is dead!" Andrea gritted her teeth.

"Oh, I'm sorry." The lady looked taken aback. "Please, accept my—"

"Okay. Fine. I'll talk to my solicitor."

The clerk nodded. "This is the best thing to do."

Andrea had nothing else to do but to leave the bank with empty hands.

"The damn solicitor!" She slammed the car's door shut. "What game is he playing?"

She pulled the phone out of her handbag and dialled the number.

"I need to speak with Mr Abrams. It's urgent," she barked when the solicitor's secretary picked up the call.

A few minutes had passed before she heard the familiar cold voice: "How can I help you, Miss Zissman?"

"The box is empty. What the hell is going on?"

Mr Abrams replied nothing. It seemed like the news struck him as much as Andrea. "Whatever was in the box, somebody removed it from there." He exhaled finally. "Somebody who had a key. Or… " He paused. "The authority to remove it without one."

"You're talking riddles. I'm tired of it," Andrea almost shouted. "What was in the bloody box?"

"I have no idea." Mr Abrams's voice remained calm. "If your mother would have liked to disclose it to me, she wouldn't have put it in the deposit box. She would've just given it to me together with the envelope."

Andrea raised her voice, "I don't know what kind of a game you're playing, but I make you talk. I'll go to the police. I'll go to the court if needed. I'll—"

"You can drag me to the court but let me tell you something first." Mr Abrams's voice sounded calm but tired. "Your mother loved you very much, she believed in you. Her only wish was to protect you."

"Did my mother tell you all that?"

"She didn't." The solicitor sighed. "Sometimes the words mean nothing. As for the instructions, she left me notes to contact you."

Andrea wanted to ask something else, but Mr Abrams cut her off. "My job here is done. Good luck with your search for the answers, Miss Zissman, and goodbye." He hung up the phone.

***

Back home, Andrea made a cup of tea and stared outside at the sleepy garden. The days became shorter and shorter, and darkness covered the naked trees with its dull greyish veil. The air was cool and damp, but Andrea didn't feel cold. In her recent financial situation, where she needed to save money on everything, including the central heating, she had started to get used to the cold. "What can be worse than a job loss?" she'd asked herself a month ago. She'd been so naïve!

She turned away from the garden. Now, the wrinkled, yellowed envelope was the only link that connected her to her past. She flipped through the notepad's pages again and again. The mountain must be in the French Alps where an avalanche killed her father. The last days her parents spent together, the last place, which stuck in her mother's mind, making her repeat it again and again. The eagle? Gabi? Gabriella? Gabriel? Her grandmother never mentioned anybody called Gabi, although Andrea wasn't surprised.

Grandma didn't like to talk about her father. She despised him so badly that when she'd become Andrea's only guardian, she gave her granddaughter her surname - Zissman.

I wonder how many secrets Grandma took to the grave with her. Andrea smirked.

She shuffled through the rest of the pages. The dark silhouettes of people, turning into shapeless shadows, the endless snowy fields with the lonely peak in the background - it was something evil and disturbing in her mother's last drawings.

Then, she noticed two pictures stuck to the notepad's cover. She separated them carefully.

One picture was a wedding photo that captured a bride and a groom surrounded by their guests. Andrea was examining the faces, trying to find her grandma or somebody she might've met before. Nobody. The longer she had been staring at her mother's white gown, the more she realised that... the bride looked heavily pregnant.

The second photo, or better to say half of it, revealed a figure of a tall man in his late thirties dressed in a ski suit. Andrea recognised the deep, grey eyes and the straight nose - the features she inherited from her father. The endless, snowy landscape transformed into a weird, lonely mountain on the horizon where it joined the greyish sky. There was another figure in the picture next to him. A child of no more than three or four years old. Andrea squinted, trying to discern if the child was a boy or a girl, but the quality of eighties' photos was poor. Old, cheap paper faded long ago, leaving wishy-washy patches.

The tiny figure was dressed in a navy-blue ski suit and a funny blue fluffy hat, which made it look like an astronaut who landed somewhere on a deserted, frozen planet. They held a cuddly toy lion clasped in a tiny hand.

Most likely, it's a boy. She continued examining the photo. On the back of the picture, she could distinguish her mother's writing - faded but still visible was the year 1985 - the same year her dad died in the avalanche.

A brother? What happened to him? Where's the second half of the picture? She tossed the photos onto the table and leaned back in her chair. She closed her eyes, but the picture of the little astronaut emerged in front of her.

"Any other members of your family… Somebody who had the authority to remove it without the key," the solicitor's words sounded in her ears.

The empty deposit box flashed in her mind. Who and why did it? What was her mother hiding her whole life?

***

The next morning, Andrea visited one of the city's archives. She knew her father worked at one of the London universities where he gave lectures on astrophysics, but she couldn't imagine that his name was so well-known in scientific circles in the late seventies and early eighties. The endless articles in different newspapers, interviews, speculations, controversies, theories...

A Solar Storm as a Source of Endless Energy.

Aurora Borealis. The Lethal Weapon of the Future.

"We can harvest the Northern Lights' energy," the British scientist claims.

She tried to read at least one of the articles, but endless formulae and the scientific terms she tripped on, annoyed her to death.

She continued to look through the papers. One of the documents caught her attention. It looked like a partially declassified file.

"What? An intelligence service?" she whispered.

Most of the document, dated from the late nineties, was redacted, however, it mentioned her father's research. According to the file, Dr Owen was involved in an expedition to the north of Iceland in 1985, aimed at studying the Aurora Borealis phenomenon. The file claimed the scientist had been living in one of the Icelandic islands for several months. The rest of the document disclosed neither the names of the other scientists who participated in the expedition nor the exact places they visited. Finally, Andrea decided that she needed a more straightforward approach and entered random words from the document into the search field in hopes of finding something more than just one inaccessible file.

Dr George Owen, Aurora Borealis, Iceland, 1985, expedition, solar energy

She scrolled through the browser's pages, slowly losing hope, then... Bang! A whole website with articles, photos, interviews, and videos appeared. Andrea was not the only one digging into it. The research and the mysterious death of her father were a subject of interest for many people. The site belonged to a French-born British journalist, Leon Callais, who led an investigation and even tried to film a documentary a couple of years ago called *Project Nothung. The Nazis' Lethal Legacy,* which caused a storm of indignation in the press.

Mr Callais built his theory on the belief that during World War II Nazi scientists created the so-called *Wunderwaffe* or *Nothung*, a device, which they wanted to use as a super weapon. However, the journalist went even further in his speculations, trying to persuade the public that *Nothung* was able to open a portal into a different dimension where the Führer and the leaders of the Third Reich had successfully escaped after the war was lost for them. Crazy as it sounded, Mr Callais claimed that the device was hidden on one of the islands in the Norwegian Sea, not far from the coast of Iceland. Struggling to prove his theory, Mr Callais didn't hesitate to suggest that the secret base on Midgardur Island, situated about twenty-five miles northwest of the Icelandic coast, still existed in the form of a colony. The colonists, the descendants of German and Icelandic soldiers, had kept its secrets all these years, protecting *Nothung* and waiting for their Führer to return. Soon, they realised that *Nothung* needed some power to return their leaders. In 1985, Dr Owen appeared to study the energy of the Aurora Borealis.

Andrea closed the page and released a deep sigh. The Nazis, the secret project, Hitler, a military base in Iceland, a parallel universe. What the hell was it all about?

***

Returning home, Andrea continued her investigation. As she expected, the journalist's social media page became a proper battlefield for all kinds of users - from World War II history amateurs to writers who claimed deep knowledge of the subject. Some opponents called Mr Callais a liar, others - a bullshit-teller who had no understanding of what he was talking about. The most furious ones claimed the journalist was a neo-Nazi sympathiser. Some Icelandic social activists sounded offended, the most radical of them demanded to ban the scandalous journalist from visiting the country to continue his investigation.

Andrea sighed and shut her laptop. She closed her eyes, leaned back on the chair. The little funny astronaut, surrounded by the sea of snow, flashed in her mind. The solicitor's last words didn't let her go.

Maybe this clown-journalist will be able to shed some light.
She opened her laptop again and started to type an email. She introduced herself briefly and asked whether he would be interested in talking to her. Just a short message, a few polite explanatory sentences, then traditional:

Kind regards,
Andrea Owen

Owen? Why did she sign it *Owen*? To attract the journalist's attention? She had always been Andrea Zissman. Always. Maybe she didn't want to be anymore?

***

The journalist's bright eyes, the colour of ocean waves, stared at Andrea, challenging her decision.

"Listen, Miss Owen. I've made it all the way from Plymouth to see you and to listen to your story. Now, when we're so close to the answers we both desperately need, you're telling me you don't want to go to Iceland?" Mr Callais frowned. "Please, don't waste my time. I'm dying for a cigarette." He shot a glance outside the hotel's lounge.

"Fifth for the last hour." Andrea snorted. "I didn't expect such a turn. I hope you understand my hesitation. I hardly know you and…" She shrugged. "After all, I can't just drop everything and go somewhere. God knows for how long, with a stranger. Why should I trust you?"

"I don't need your trust." Mr Callais grinned and finished his coffee in one gulp. "You just have no other options but to trust me if you want to know the truth about your family. You won't fish out anything from the solicitor, even if he knows more than he tells you, although I doubt he does. Whoever emptied the deposit box meant serious business."

She looked into his eyes, trying to find the real person behind the dazzling visage. She expected him to be older, but he looked about her age. With his dark, short, spiky hair, dyed platinum blond on the ends, with an extravagant watch, dressed in a leather jacket and jeans, Mr Callais looked more like some scandalous TV-show celebrity than a high-profile journalist.

"Do you think I'm in danger now?" She squinted.

He shrugged. "I don't know. The only thing is clear - somebody wants to prevent you from finding something your mother had been hiding her whole life. If my theory is correct—"

"Your theory is full of controversies. And you know that." She shook her head. "The only evidence that led you to Iceland is pictures of *Standartenführer* Otto von Koch, the authenticity of which has never been proven. What makes you think, apart from these photos, that we need to go there? As far as I remember, Iceland declared neutrality during the war and—"

"To be neutral doesn't necessarily mean to be friendly to the allies." The journalist shrugged.

"Oh. Do you understand that all you have as proof are just well-known war stories and a couple of photos of poor quality? The photo you claimed was taken on an Icelandic island, for example. You can't even confirm that the person in it is Otto von Koch. The man turned his back to the camera. How can you prove that this is the same SS-officer filmed in Berlin and then in Kristiansand?" Andrea shook her head.

"I'm sure *Nothung* is still there as well as the colony called 'Aurora.'. You read my works."

"Even if 'Aurora' exists, why does nobody know about it? In your articles, you're talking about some kind of strange cult that the colonists worship."

"Yes, but their 'religion' is only a cover for what they really do there." He moved closer, lowering his voice. "Weapons sales, bribes to authorities, money fraud, kidnapping, maybe forced labour, maybe even torture - the list is not long enough to describe what's going on in the colony. 'Aurora' has so much power and influence because the

Nazi gold can buy everybody in the government and help to hush up lots of things."

Andrea didn't know what to say.

Feeling her hesitation, he switched on his laptop and, without saying a word, showed her a scan of an old photo.

Andrea gasped. "Where did you get that?"

It was a picture of her father in a ski suit in the middle of an iced dessert. She could swear the photo was taken at the same time as the one she'd gotten. Even the landscape - the valley and the bizarre-shaped lonely mountain - looked similar, but this time, the mountain seemed much closer.

"This is from the declassified files," he explained. "I compared it to the photo and your mother's drawings you sent me. The analysis of both pictures confirms that they were taken at the same time, in the same place. This mountain…" He pointed his long, thin finger to the scan. "It matches only one place in Europe, and it is not in the French Alps." He made a meaningful pause. "In fact, it's not even a mountain. It's the peak of Madgarjokull volcano on Midgardur Island. Your father and Otto von Koch had been there. Dr Owen knew that the island was the best place for Aurora watching and studying. He made a mistake though, coming too close to the colony's secrets."

Andrea nodded slowly. "The drawings of the eagle make sense now."

"You contacted me. That makes me think that you're as interested in discovering the truth as I am. These people killed your father, intimidated your family, robbed you of vital evidence. You've got an opportunity to find out what happened to your father. Please, help me. Please, help yourself."

His last words resonated in her heart. *Maybe Mr Callais is right?* She shifted in her chair.

"What do you do for a living, by the way?" he asked, breaking the awkward pause, leaning back in the hotel's wide chair. "Do you need to take leave from work or something?"

"I don't work at the moment. I've been laid-off." She waved her hand.

He beamed. "It makes our mission even easier. The tickets are on me or, better to say, on my employers. These greedy bastards expect a sensational story so they need to pay."

"Wait. I'm not going anywhere." Andrea almost jumped from her chair. "I thought you could shed some light on my father's death. I didn't know you were going to drag me to Iceland."

"I can't do it on my own." Mr Callais shook his head. "Besides, what are you going to do? Just sit here and wait when I bring you the truth on a plate?"

"I'm not going to sit and wait. I'll contact the embassy to provide me with the information from the police archives. There should be something about my father and brother there." Andrea shrugged. "Some reports of missing people or something."

"The information about your father's research is still classified." Mr Callais smirked. "Who would report your father's disappearance to the local police? Your mother? I doubt it."

"Two people can't just vanish."

Mr Callais sighed. "Good luck with your inquiry then." He put his business card on the table and rose, ready to leave. "Give me a call if you manage to get something from the embassy. I doubt it, though."

***

The next day, Andrea didn't waste time and called the embassy first thing in the morning. After a couple of attempts to get through to the right department, she was finally redirected to the National Commissioner of the Police office.

"Do you have any documents, for example, your brother's birth certificate or passport, to prove that you're related?" the secretary asked her after Andrea finished her story.

"No. I've told you already. All I have is his photo as a child."

"Do you have any confirmation from the British police that the case of your father's disappearance in Iceland has been closed?"

Andrea swallowed her emotions back. "But the case doesn't even exist. Nobody reported my father and brother as missing persons." *Let alone my father's research in Iceland is still classified.* "I thought that the case can be opened if I—"

"Then, I'm afraid we can't help you, Miss Zissman," the secretary's voice sounded unapologetically. "The only way the Commissioner is going to look into it is the official request from the British police."

"If I come to Iceland in person," Andrea insisted, "to the local police station in Akureyri, maybe they'll be able to help me."

"You'll just waste your time. I'm sorry to say, but your relatives went missing over thirty years ago. Your request is not enough to start the investigation."

Andrea said goodbye and hung up the phone. "Damn!" She poured already cold coffee from the jar and went outside in the still dark garden.

A shy, thin veil of snow had covered the trees and shrubs, turning the garden into a winter wonderland.

She inhaled the frosty air and caught herself thinking how it was in Iceland now. Cold, snowy, and unwelcoming? She closed her eyes and tried to imagine deep snowdrifts, sparkling under the midnight sun, the flat peak of Madgarjokull volcano on the low horizon, the sky, deep and cold… Had she visited the island with her father and brother? These images. Were they her real memories or just snippets of what she saw in the photos and her mother's drawings? Gabi. The name flashed in her mind, and she released a deep sigh. Where could she find them?

She went back to the warmth of the living room. The loud ping of an incoming email brought her back from her reverie. She took a seat back at the desk and opened the email.

Oh, another 'no'. She sighed, reading a polite generic reply from one of the dozens of employers she'd sent her CV. She deleted the email and stared into space for a few minutes, then picked up her phone and dialled the number.

"Good morning," Mr Callais greeted her.

"I'm sorry if I woke you up, but—"

"Ah, don't worry. I'm an early bird. At least today." He chuckled. "I guess your investigation led you nowhere. I warned you that dealing with Icelandic authorities is a waste of time."

"That's what they told me at the National Commissioner's office," Andrea mumbled, annoyed. "I think that if we go together to their archives and request the information, then… You're an accredited journalist, after all. They can't refuse—"

"I'm afraid my accreditation doesn't lead me that far. I can't demand anything from the foreign authorities if they don't want to cooperate." He paused. "You know they're right about all these long bureaucratic procedures. They'll take forever and may never be successful."

"Mr Callais…" She paused. "What am I supposed to do?"

"I think you already know the answer." He lowered his voice. "And please, call me Leon."

***

After a three-hour flight from London to Reykjavik and an almost five-hour drive to Akureyri, Andrea started to feel like their journey would never end. So bizarre, so surreal, like a nightmare, like a heavy narcotic dream. During three days of waiting for the tickets and hotel booking confirmation from Leon, she cursed herself thousands of times, struggling to believe she agreed to take part in this "adventure". And now, she was sitting in the car with this clown, a self-proclaimed investigator, whom she'd met less than a week before. They'd been driving to nowhere, chasing some mystical group of neo-Nazis. *What the fuck am I doing here?* The memory of the empty deposit box and her mother's drawings haunted her at night, though. Deep in her soul, she knew she needed to come here.

"I've booked a room for one night in a B&B on the outskirts of Akureyri." Leon pulled her out of her reverie. "I feel absolutely exhausted. We need a rest after such a long day. Tomorrow morning, the ferry will bring us to the island."

"You... you what? Have you booked only one room?"

"We're a couple of photographers who came to film the Aurora. Forgot?" He frowned. "Don't you think it's illogical if a couple stays in different rooms?"

"Logic has never been my strongest point."

"As well as rational thinking," he mumbled.

"I hope you've booked a room with twin beds, at least."

"I tried, but they couldn't guarantee it."

"Shame." She chuckled. "You'll need either to move the beds or sleep on the floor."

Their heated conversation had been interrupted by the SatNav, announcing their destination was in front of them. The three-storey greyish B&B looked tidy and welcoming like everything in Iceland. A smiling blonde girl at the reception desk checked them in and handed out their room keys.

Andrea dropped her suitcase and went to the shower, leaving Leon to sort the beds out.

The darkness covered the city in a matter of minutes, and very soon the tired winter sun disappeared below the horizon, and the city lit up its lights.

"They started to put up Christmas decorations, just like in England." Andrea smiled when she appeared from the bathroom.

"I thought you celebrated Hanukkah, not Christmas."

She shrugged. "My grandma tried hard to get me into it, but I always preferred Christmas."

Their room was on the second floor, opening out to a view of the harbour and the mountains, rising as gloomy masses on the fading horizon. Their snowy peaks were still visible. The night was cold and clear. The city sounded quiet. Its nightlife was prepared for the holiday season. There were not many high buildings there, so nothing obstructed the view.

"I don't bother about Christmas." Leon sat on his bed, staring into the dark masses of the mountains.

A warm, rich smell of coffee filled up the room. As soon as Leon had learned that smoking was prohibited in the hotel, he had no other entertainment but a cup of strong coffee.

"You don't celebrate it?" Andrea frowned. "Oh, I mean… aren't you a Christian? Or just don't practice? I mean I'm sorry if—"

"My father left me and my mum on Christmas Eve," he murmured. "I was only seven."

She sat next to him. "Oh, I'm sorry. I wish my parents would've been with me every Christmas, but you know my story."

"Then, a couple of years later, there was Christmas in England, with a new English 'dad', with two English stepbrothers, whom I barely could understand, and who absolutely hated me."

"Ah, that's why you came to England." Andrea nodded.

"Yeah. It was a painful experience for a nine-year-old . When my little sister was born, I became a heavy burden for my new family. My stepfather locked me up in a boarding school from which I escaped twice. I ran to London, hoping to return to France, and got into trouble. Oh, God! That was my protest against my new family and new country." He chuckled, taking a big sip of coffee. "Now, you know who I really am. A rebel."

She shrugged. "I'm a bit jealous."

"Jealous?"

"Well, at least you know the truth about your family. I feel like I've been surrounded by lies my entire life. First, Grandma, now... I've found out that my mother lied to me as well, faking her mental health issues."

"You've got a chance to change everything now." He smiled. "Your trip here is your chance."

She didn't reply, just waved.

"Sorry, I've misjudged you." She sighed after a prolonged pause. "You're a strong person. You pulled yourself together. You didn't give up. You started to do what you always wanted to."

"A strong person? I wouldn't call it 'strong'. I was kicked out three times from three different universities for my behaviour. In fact, I didn't want to study at all. I started to study journalism for one purpose only - to piss off my parents. They wanted me to study law, social sciences, or some other boring bullshit. I was all into history and writing, so I rebelled again. When the faculty organised one of these boring end-of-year parties, I turned out dressed as an SS officer. Nobody appreciated my joke, including my parents."

Andrea chuckled. "Did you confuse it with Halloween?"

He had no time to reply, as a round white cloud growing in the sky above the harbour attracted his and Andrea's attention.

He came closer to the window and opened it. "Switch off the light, please."

Andrea held her breath. "Is it…? Is that what I think it is?"

The cloud was growing bigger and bigger, turning almost spherical, then falling apart into three smaller pieces.

"On such a cold clear night, the display should be good." Leon clapped his hands and pulled his SLR camera out of the suitcase.

On the opposite side of the hotel, a few people came out of the restaurant with their cameras and phones ready for the show.

The clouds started to move around in some weird roundelay and, the next second, the whole sky exploded with bright green dancing ribbons. The ribbons turned into huge waving sheets. Bright green, yellow, white, and purple - the skies were on fire. The sheets were swirling and folding, creating mystical flowers and birds, and even something that looked like an angel. The angel waved its wide wings and fell apart into vertical ribbons pierced by thin white rays.

"I've never seen anything like that in my life," Andrea whispered as if she was afraid her voice could scare the lights.

Leon grinned. "Do you still regret coming here?"

The show finished as unexpectedly as it had started.

"We might see it again later tonight," he said.

"You told me Midgardur Island is one of the best places for Aurora watching."

"That's why *Nothung* is there." He nodded. "The Aurora Borealis here is the result of the collision between particles, which are brought by the solar storms to Earth's atmosphere."

"Do you mean my father discovered how to extract the energy from the Aurora and—"

"Well, I think he was pretty close to it." Leon shrugged. "Originally, some kind of radioactive substance was used to power *Nothung*. According to the files, it could've been red mercury. People who worked on the project suffered from severe dizziness and other strange symptoms. Some of them even died from the exposure. To make the device work properly, the colonists found an alternative fuel - the power of the solar storms."

"Sounds like science fiction to me." She shrugged, too exhausted to comprehend the scientific terms.

"All evidences lead to Midgardur." Leon shook his head. "In 1939, long before the British forces arrived, Germany sent an expedition to build a clandestine weather station on one of the northern islands. This island covered in glaciers and lava fields became an ideal place for hiding a submarine, carrying the Nazi gold and *Nothung*."

Andrea sunk into the chair and closed her eyes. "I hope we'll soon find out."

***

"What made you come here, guys?" a blond ferryman asked them in English, smiling sincerely, when his tiny ferry made a turn to leave the harbour.

Apart from the old sailor, they were alone aboard.

"The tourists don't often go much farther than Akureyri," he added.

"We're photographers." Leon pointed to his heavy camera with a massive lens. "We're chasing the Aurora all over the world to take the best photos. We've been to Norway, Finland, Alaska, even Russia."

"We've heard Midgardur Island is the best place in the north of Iceland for the lights' display," Andrea said.

"Ah, that's true." The ferryman touched his grey beard. "The lights are magnificent here. People are not so great, though."

"What do you mean?"

Leon and Andrea exchanged worried looks.

"Just unsocial, not very friendly. I've been working here for several years. They never said a word apart from traditional greetings. I love to chat with my passengers, you know. But these guys are... Ah, just sitting on their island, being completely cut off from the world." He waved. "They could've made a fortune on Aurora watching tours, but they're too lazy."

They kept silent for a while. The ferry was getting closer to the island, and the dark mystical silhouette of the Madgarjokull volcano rose up to the bright azure sky.

Andrea distinguished a few multicoloured bungalows nesting on the gloomy lava rocks like a flock of puffins.

"Midgardur Village," Leon whispered.

"Your guesthouse is on the other side, in the centre of the settlement," the ferryman said. "They only have one, anyway. You won't be mistaken. Rent a snowmobile when you arrive. It'll be easier to get around the glacier."

Something heavy pressed on Andrea's soul. It was a strange, inexplicable melancholy, untold, unwept sorrow of something that was lost long ago. What was it? She didn't know. This uninhabited but solemn landscape, this ice-cold gusty wind, these greyish stormy waters brought memories that never existed.

"Are you alright?" Leon touched her sleeve. "You turn so pale."

"I'm fine. It's just so weird, so... I feel like—"

"Like what? Like you've been here? Like déjà-vu?"

"No, no. It doesn't matter," she mumbled.

The ferry had started to manoeuvre for the mooring, and a few minutes later, they were saying goodbye to the ferryman.

"Be careful, guys," the sailor replied.

Leon waved his hand. "Thanks."

Snowdrifts covered the sharp black stones of the shore, but a path leading to the village was cleaned. The villagers used it to get to the ferry, which took them, their vehicles, post, and goods to Akureyri and back twice a day. The path ran slightly uphill, opening to a mind-blowing view of a volcanic beach with its bizarre vertical formations of rocks that looked like black flames turned into stones in the blue background of the sunny sky. The traditional village had only a few dozen one- or two-storey houses. The one main street led to a central square that lurked in the valley at the bottom of the glacier.

At the outskirts of the settlement, some kind of industrial zone appeared - a few long, low buildings that looked like warehouses, a power station, and even a helipad.

Andrea mentioned that it looked out of place here.

"The strangest thing of all is that none of these industrial buildings can be found on any online maps." Leon nodded, taking out his small binoculars and examining the industrial zone.

"Why?"

He shrugged. "That's what we're going to find out."

***

As expected, the only guesthouse on the island was situated in the centre of the village. Moving through the ankle-deep snow, Leon and Andrea agreed a snowmobile was the best transport option. The narrow streets looked deserted.

"Everybody's working," the hostess of the guesthouse explained without a smile when Leon tried to start a conversation.

It turned out they were the only guests there. The hostess, a large unsmiling lady of an uncertain age, checked Andrea's passport, explained the rules, and handed them the keys. Leon decided it would be safer not to attract attention by providing his details and booking the room on Andrea's name.

"Your room is upstairs, the first one to the left." The lady nodded to the stairs. "Call reception if you need something." No smile again. Not even a slight shadow of it.

"Ah, we'd like to rent a snowmobile," Leon said, picking up his and Andrea's suitcases. "We've been told that it's the most popular vehicle here."

"Do you have a valid licence?"

"We both do."

"Okay. It'll be delivered to the entrance in about an hour."

Andrea nodded. "Thank you." She walked a few steps up, following Leon, when a powerful underground tremor shook the spiral staircases.

"What was that?" She grabbed the rail and pushed Leon in the back slightly so they wouldn't end up on the floor.

"Ah, the volcano awakens." The hostess waved. "It became active a few months ago and—"

The next push made her grab the reception desk, and the alarms of the cars parked nearby drowned out her words.

"We're used to such things here." For the first time, she beamed her perfect wide smile.

Leon and Andrea exchanged anxious looks, but didn't say anything and continued their way upstairs.

"Ah, finally…" Leon opened the window and lit a cigarette after they arrived at their room and unpacked the suitcases.

There was not a hint of a fire alarm. In fact, the whole room looked dated - the furniture from the late eighties, the worn-out carpet, the faded curtains of an unidentified colour that, most likely, were dark purple many years ago, and a few chipped tiles in the bathroom.

Everything was surprisingly clean, though. The bathroom smelled of bleach, and the towels dazzled with ideal whiteness.

They didn't bother much about comfort. Leon looked happy to be able to smoke in the room, whereas Andrea was mesmerised by the sea view and the volcano. Its flat peak dominated the island's landscape.

The unsettling feeling came back to her and swallowed all other emotions, producing a mix of sadness, anxiety, hope, and excitement.

"What is that?" Andrea pointed to the mountain. "At first, I thought it was a cloud, but—"

Leon turned in the same direction. "It's smoke. If my theory is correct, the energy of *Nothung* can destabilise the magnetic fields and lead to Madgarjokull's activity. I don't believe in coincidences. This volcano has been asleep for centuries."

"Sooner or later, it may cause an eruption. What will happen to the village and its people?"

"By then, the device will be fully charged, and its power will be equal to thousands of volcanoes. It's more than enough to destroy not only this tiny island, but the whole country."

Andrea swallowed her growing anxiety back, but said nothing.

"The sky is clear today." Leon squinted, taking a long puff and staring somewhere beyond the horizon. "It's a good night for 'harvesting'."

She followed his look. "Of course, Madgarjokull. You can't imagine a better place for it."

Leon clapped his hands. "Ah, our transport is here." He pointed down to the car park, where a guy was handing a snowmobile key to their unfriendly hostess.

"I think we need to make a loop around the village and decide where we should start our search," Andrea said.

"We need to find some kind of bar first. I'm dying for coffee. I doubt we can expect it from our hostess."

They put on their coats and went downstairs. After a brief argument, Andrea finally agreed to sit in the back seat of their snowmobile and allowed Leon to drive since he claimed that he had done it before.

"Should I hold these handles on the back?" she asked, putting on her helmet. She had never been an extreme sports fan, nor had she ridden a snowmobile or even a bike before. The helmet felt uncomfortable and heavy. The vehicle looked unstable.

Leon winked. "You can hold them or you can hold me."

"Piss off!" She grabbed the handles.

A few seconds later, she realised that she'd made a mistake when Leon revved the engine, and the snowmobile pulled forward so hard that she almost lost her balance. The blast of the icy wind punched her in the face, burning her skin with its cold fury. Despite the helmet, her eyes started to water, and her nose ran. She could hardly see anything. "Oh! Damn! What are you doing? Stop it!"

The snowmobile was drifting and bumping, and Andrea had already run out of swear words. Leon found it hilarious and didn't intend to slow down.

"Stop it!" she screamed when the snowmobile turned round the corner and, losing her balance, she almost fell off.

"What's wrong? I suggested that you hold my waist." Leon slowed down and parked at the entrance of a café. "I did no more than fifty kilometres per hour."

"You should've done less in a built-up area. You could've hit somebody," she continued, pulling off the uncomfortable helmet.

"This village is almost uninhabited. The streets are empty. Let's be honest, you're more concerned about yourself."

"What? Bullshit!"

He only chuckled, then opened the door and entered the warmth of the café.

The place was small but cosy, with wooden panels on the walls and beams criss-crossing the ceiling. They were the first customers, so a barman put aside the book he'd been reading and greeted them in Icelandic.

"Could we... eh... have coffee, please?" Leon started slowly, unsure whether the guy understood English.

"Of course, you can." The barman beamed. "Espresso? Latte? Cappuccino?"

They ordered their drinks and took a seat. The monotonous buzz of a coffee machine drowned out all other sounds. The whole place filled with the warm, mildly bitter smell of freshly ground coffee beans.

The door opened, and a new guest entered the room. Dressed in a black jacket and black ski-type trousers, the tall man nodded to the barman in greeting. He took a seat next to the guys' table, and without taking off his sunglasses, focused on his phone.

The barman brought them their order, then went to the man. They exchanged a few words in Icelandic. The man wore sunglasses, yet Andrea could feel his heavy look on her back.

"This guy is watching us. I feel it," she whispered when the man had been distracted by the arrival of his meal.

Leon nodded. "I agree. He's suspiciously early for lunch."

"Let's finish our coffee and discuss our plans outside."

Leon looked a bit disappointed but followed her advice. Saying goodbye to the barman, they were on the way out when the ground jerked, then again and again. The glasses clinked on shelves behind the bar, the low brass shades swayed, the entire building vibrated, and the barman hurried to protect the bottles containing alcohol.

Andrea screamed, and the man in a black jacket swore, as half of his soup spilled all over his trousers.

"Madgarjokull is getting angry today." The barman squeezed an apologetic smile.

"Maybe it just doesn't like unexpected guests," the tall man replied in perfect English.

***

They made a circle around the village so Andrea could get used to the ride. She pressed her shoulders against Leon's back and gripped his waist to shield herself from the wind. She expected him to smell of cigarette smoke like every heavy smoker she knew. He didn't. It was the smell of some spicy aftershave, mint, strong espresso, salty sea breeze from the shore, danger, adventure, freedom...

They left the village and headed north towards the mysterious industrial zone. The snowmobile slid across the endless white valley of the glacier. It went more than seventy kilometres, but Andrea didn't feel the speed now. The icy surface of the glacier was ideally smooth. She closed her eyes for a second, and again the unknown feeling drowned her. She saw this valley with her eyes closed, or, better to say, she felt as if she'd already known this place.

Leon stopped on the top of a hill.

"There's no point in getting closer. The cameras are everywhere." He took the helmet off and rose from his seat.

The road went downhill and wriggled like a gigantic albino snake through the valley, ending up at a spacious but busy car park full of snowmobiles, jeeps on huge high wheels, and even two so-called super trucks - massive heavy lorries, designed specifically for crawling on the icy roads. Behind the parking lot, a few warehouse-looking buildings stood surrounded by a dull concrete fence. Such serious security measures looked even more suspicious in the middle of nowhere.

"It looks like a restricted area. We can't just randomly walk in," Andrea said. "What are we supposed to do?"

"You underestimated me." Leon grinned and took his backpack out of the boot's rack. He opened a black plastic case. "I've got my spy with me." He nodded to the case and put together a tiny drone with a micro-camera and a remote control.

It looked more like something between a toy helicopter and a big metal dragonfly. Leon switched it on, and "the dragonfly" made a circle around Andrea's head.

"Cute!" She smiled and stretched out her palm, and Leon landed it on her hand.

"I hope this little cutie can get through where we can't." He switched the drone back on again.

Despite its small size, it was fast and could fly high, which made it invisible to CCTV. Leon navigated it without difficulty.

He's used to spying. Andrea chuckled.

Soon, "the dragonfly" disappeared behind the fence, and she switched her attention to the screen.

"Aha, there are security guards inside." Leon nodded at the screen. "Just as I thought."

The drone took a couple of photos, then turned around and flew to the nearest warehouse. It hovered in front of a narrow, dusty window, and Leon and Andrea could distinguish endless rows of wooden boxes with numbers on them. A couple of men in high-visibility jackets and helmets wandered through the labyrinth of boxes, counting and inputting something on their tablets.

In the opposite corner of the building, two workers messed around with a forklift. One driver looked inexperienced, as the machine jerked back and forth, strugling to lift a pallet of stacked boxes. His colleague gesticulated frantically, trying to direct the forklift, but all his efforts were in vain. The two watched on the screen as the pallet cracked, and all the boxes fell, scattering their contents across the floor. The driver's colleague was lucky to jump away just in time to avoid an injury.

"God! This is…" Andrea murmured.

"This is the weapon." Leon nodded. "Guns, machine guns, bullets."

"There's enough here to supply a whole army."

"Let's have a look at another building."

The next moment, a loud female voice called out from behind them. Two people in black uniforms came closer. A tall, rather large woman with very short blonde hair asked them something in Icelandic. A man kept silent, but he looked familiar. Andrea recognised the café's regular customer.

"Hi, umg… Sorry, we don't speak Icelandic," Leon started.

"What are you doing here?" the man asked without a greeting. He took his sunglasses off, and his pale grey eyes burned with their frosty indignation.

"We're photographers. We came here to film the Aurora and the wildlife."

"There was a fantastic display in Akureyri yesterday night," Andrea's voice trembled. "We've been told that Midgardur Island is the best place for the lights' watching, so we hoped that today—"

"It's only one o'clock in the afternoon. Don't you think it's a bit too early for Aurora?" The man grinned, and his colleague chuckled in agreement.

"This land is private property," the woman said. "You need to leave as soon as possible."

Andrea made the last attempt, "Why can't we—"

"Because the owner of this property doesn't want you to be here. Leave or we'll force you,' the man snapped.

Andrea and Leon had nothing to do but turn to the village.

"Damn!" Leon revved the engine. "We left the drone there."

"What could we do? Even if they don't find it, they'll be watching us. We need to be careful."

"I think we need to go somewhere quiet and make a new plan." With that said, he turned the snowmobile and headed to the beach.

***

They parked the snowmobile on a cliff and took steps down to the black sands of the beach. The sun was ready to sink into the sea - scarlet-red and eery. The short polar day descended into the greyish twilight of the long polar night.

As they reached the bottom of the steps, Andrea noticed a wisp of thin white smoke, rising from the ground. The air filled with the smell of sulphur.

"That's due to the underground hot springs," Leon said. "They're close to the surface. That's why there is no snow on the beach." He touched the sand. "It's so warm." He smiled and took a seat on a big shard of volcanic rock with fancy edges that made it look like a gothic throne. He pulled off his hiking boots and buried his pale feet into the warm sand. "I need a bit of spa after such a stressful morning. I'm freezing after that ride on the glacier."

Andrea smiled and followed his example. This improvised spa relaxed her a little bit, and they kept silent for a while.

"You have big feet." She noticed when Leon had started to wipe the sand off of them to put his shoes on.

"Oh, thank you. I'll take it as a compliment." He chuckled, but she pushed him slightly, and he slid down from his stone throne.

They kept silent.

"I'm scared," she broke the pause first. "You were right. This place is dangerous, these people are dangerous."

"I'm sorry I dragged you into it, but it was the only way to make you believe me." He took her hands in his, looking into her eyes. "This is the only way to find out the truth about your family."

"Please, tell me we'll be okay."

"I can't guarantee you that." He touched her cheek, wiping away a tiny tear.

He wanted to tell her something else, but froze in place when a quiet, high-pitched voice had sounded from somewhere behind the nearest rocks. Andrea calmed down as well. The voice continued to sing, coming closer and closer.

"It's German." Leon's face turned pale. "Oh, God! It's... It's a..."

He didn't finish as the next second the singer himself appeared from behind the rocks. A boy, about six or seven years old, dressed in a long navy-blue jacket and a bright red hat, carried a shabby wicker basket with small pieces of rock in it. He had stopped singing when he noticed he wasn't alone. His little round face with its tiny button nose looked anxious and curious at the same time.

"Hey, buddy!" Leon smiled. "What are you doing here? Don't be afraid. We won't harm you."

The boy didn't reply. He clutched his basket and prepared to run away.

"I'm Andrea. Andrea." Andrea repeated twice, deciding that the little stranger might not understand English.

"This is Leon." She pointed to the journalist. "Are you alone here? Where are your parents or your teacher?"

"I'm Rufus." The boy took one step closer. "I have no parents. I live in the Grey House with the other kids."

Leon and Andrea exchanged curious looks.

"Are you from INTERPOL or something?" Rufus continued in English, which sounded impressive for his age.

"Oh, no, no." Leon chuckled. "We're photographers. We came here to film the lights and the animals – birds, whales, everything."

"There were lots of seals on this beach. Sometimes, they used to come here with their white babies." Rufus nodded, smiling. "I think they liked the warm sand. They knew me and allowed me to come closer."

"Oh, really? Will we have a chance to meet them?" Andrea asked.

"They won't come anymore."

"Why?"

"The Governor and his people killed them all. Even the babies." The smile vanished from his face.

"Who? The Governor? Why did he do that?" Leon asked.

"Just for fun." Rufus shrugged. "The Governor said that he would like a rug and flip-flops made from baby-seals' fur."

Andrea gritted her teeth. Leon pressed her hand as if he wanted to prevent her from asking further questions.

"You speak very good English, Rufus. We heard your German song too," he started again. "Where did you learn the languages?"

"Ah, all the kids in the Grey House speak English, but I prefer Icelandic or German." Rufus waved. "Our Governor doesn't like Icelandic, though, and Miss Richter always tells us to speak German in his presence."

"Do you sing this song with Miss Richter? Did she teach you this?"

"Yeah." Little Rufus seemed to lose his interest in them and started to collect rocks into his basket. "We should all know this song and many other things when the leaders come back," he continued.

Andrea nodded slowly. "The leaders? Oh, I see."

"Miss Richter always tells me I should work hard and behave well, so the Führer will pick me to be his special guard."

"Do you…? What? Do you collect these rocks for Miss Richter? Did she send you here?"

"No, I'm collecting them for the Governor. I'm working at his house in the afternoon after our classes and on the weekends as well. The Governor would like to build a new greenhouse with many fancy flowers, and Mrs Bromm, his housekeeper, said we needed some stones to decorate the flower beds. The volcanic rocks look better."

Leon and Andrea kept silent.

"The storm is coming. The weather changes every couple of hours here." Rufus broke an inconvenient pause. "It's not fun meeting it here." He pointed to the heavy stormy cloud. "You'd better go back to the village."

"What about you?" Leon asked. "We would've given you a lift back, but our snowmobile—"

"Don't worry. I'll use the tunnel."

"What tunnel?"

"There're lots of them here, and they are all connected. The villagers can't use them, only those who work in the Governor's house, and the Governor himself to get to the Temple of Aurora."

"Can we use these tunnels?" Andrea asked.

"Oh, no, no. And, please, don't tell anybody in the village that you talked to me." Rufus looked horrified. "I'll be punished if Mrs Bromm or Miss Richter finds out." And he hurried back to the rocks where he had appeared from.

"Wait. Wait a minute." Leon tried to catch up with him. "I swear we won't tell anybody, but please, stay with us a bit longer."

"We enjoy talking to you." Andrea nodded. "What is it – the Temple of Aurora? Have you been there?"

"I'll get into trouble because of you," the boy muttered.

Andrea patted his shoulder. "No, no. You can trust us."

"Nobody can see the Temple, only the Governor can go there. I heard that a boy from the Grey House wanted to find the secret tunnel that led to the Temple, but he lost his way and was never seen again. The Governor was furious. He shouted at us and even at Miss Richter. I was so scared that he would punish all of us."

"Punish?"

"Yes. Put us in a cell or something else. I've never been punished, but I heard lots of stories from other kids." He paused for a second, his eyes filled with tears. "I don't want to go to a cell. It's dark and cold, and full of rats and spiders. I don't want to be punished."

"You won't, Rufus." Leon knelt on one knee and took the boy's plump palm in his hand. "You're our friend now. Don't be afraid."

"You're different from the people in the village." The boy wiped his tears and smiled, but the smile was bitter. "Nobody likes me there."

"Why?"

"I don't want to be the Führer's guard. Some boys want to be like our Governor. They think he's cool, but I don't like him. He's a bad, angry man, and he scares me."

Leon shook his hand. "It was a pleasure to meet you. Take care, buddy."

They helped him to collect a full basket of rocks and watched him leave until his silhouette disappeared behind one of the rock formations.

The storm cloud reached the beach, the wind picked up, and the first prickly snowflakes filled the air, swirling in a crazy, chaotic dance. Leon and Andrea drove back to the village.

***

"This is worse than I could imagine." Leon sat on the bed scooping his fish soup, which they had ordered to be served to the room.

"I still can't believe it. A six-year-old is singing Hitlerjugend's anthem and talking about the Führer, INTERPOL, and Aurora." Andrea circled the room. "I didn't even know such words when I was six."

"No doubt, he heard them from the adults, his teacher Miss Richter, or whatever her name is, or this mysterious almighty Governor who uses little orphans as his slaves."

"You were right." She sat on the bed next to him. "Sorry, I didn't trust you."

"I wish I were wrong." He shook his head. "We haven't got serious evidence. We don't even know who we're dealing with. We've lost our drone. The testimony of a six-year-old boy won't be taken seriously, even if he agrees to speak."

"We need to find the Temple of Aurora." Andrea clenched her fists. "I think this is the key to *Nothung* and to the colony's secrets."

"I underestimated you." Leon chuckled. "Oh, I just noticed that we've got a double bed here."

"You can try to sleep on the floor, but the night could be quite chilly. Don't worry." She shrugged. "We'll fit."

Leon snorted. "Well, I think I should be worried now, after you cuddled up to me during the whole ride today."

"What? I don't even want to touch such an ashtray like you."

"Ah girl, whatever."

"I'll have a nap for an hour or so," Andrea said.

"Good idea. We'll continue our investigation at night." Leon shrugged, then opened the window and lit a cigarette.

She curled up under her blanket and closed her eyes. People, faces, places, endless snowfields, the frosty wind in her face, the sea, the sunset, Rufus with his basket, the strict face of the security guard...

Then the images changed, and she found herself in bed. She felt the light summer breeze on her face. She could see the bed's edges and the curtains on the window, and the white ceiling. She could hear a quiet dialogue. Two voices, a male and a female, were discussing something in English, but she couldn't understand a word. She had never heard the voices before. She made a move, trying to get up from the bed but struggled.

The next moment, she saw a face. A little boy stood up on a chair and bent over the edge, staring at her with a curious smile. He stretched his little hand to touch her. His dark-brown eyes with long lashes, his wavy longish hair... She saw the boy somewhere, she knew him, but she couldn't remember.

"Gabi, Gabi! Leave your sister alone," the strict female voice interrupted his gazing. "She's tired. Let her sleep, or she'll start to cry again."

Gabi? Gabi! Gabriel. My brother. She opened her mouth ready to shout, but something pushed her, turning the room upside down again and again. A cold sweat covered her forehead. She shouted and woke up in the guesthouse room.

The building had been vibrating from the underground tremors, and Leon tried to keep his balance, gathering the ash from his cigarette and the litter from a flipped over bin.

"Damn, girl! Only an earthquake can wake you up," he grumbled when the vibration had finally stopped. "You were crying in your dream."

She didn't say anything, only wrapped tightly in her blanket and went to the window. The darkness covered the island completely, the storm calmed down, and the first stars blinked with their white dull light.

He put his hand on her shoulder. "What was it? A bad dream?"

"I saw my brother. He's still alive. I'm sure," she whispered, patting his hand. All the muscles in her body relaxed.

"We'll find him, I promise."

They'd kept silent for a while, until the lights flashed in the sky like a green moving cloud, then broke down into endless waving ribbons. They were waving and swirling, changing the shades to purple, yellow, and white. Watching the lights in silence, Leon released Andrea, took out his camera, and opened the window ready to film.

Andrea broke the long pause. "Look!" She pointed to the volcano. "The lights are different there."

The ribbons transformed into a bright-purple funnel, descending from the sky and almost touching the smoking crater. It looked as if somebody had switched on a gigantic vacuum cleaner and tried to suck the Aurora into the volcano. The view was spectacular, but they had no time for enjoying it.

"Let's go," Leon said. "Hurry up! This is it. They're harvesting."

They put on their boots and jackets and left the room.

The frost came together with the darkness. Despite the storm having passed as quickly as it started, the wind from the sea was strong. The snow sounded crunchy under their feet, and their scarves were covered by a thin layer of ice.

They jumped on the snowmobile, and Leon revved the engine. A few minutes later, the streets of the village had been left far behind. They were alone with the Aurora and the endless snow fields of the glacier. The snow looked miraculously green under the unstable light of the Aurora. Leon drove at the maximum speed. The snowmobile glided through the icy desert, and the gigantic bright funnel grew closer and closer every minute. Soon, they could see what produced this effect. On the very edge of the crater, some sort of enormous solar panels were installed. They moved slowly in a synchronised rhythm, following the movement of the lights. They couldn't see them during the day, which made Andrea think they had been hidden somewhere in the mass of the rock. She snuggled tighter to Leon when she heard an engine's noise behind her. She turned around.

Five snowmobiles caught up with them. They were smaller and faster, five drivers were dressed in all black. Leon had also noticed them, but it was too late. He could not compete with the more experienced drivers or with the turbo engines of their small snowmobiles. A few seconds later, they surrounded them, circling like birds of prey. Leon made the last desperate attempt to break the circle and head for the nearest rocks. Andrea recognised the tall figure of the security guard they talked to that morning.

The next second, a gunshot struck the snowmobile's back track. Andrea screamed and lost her grip. Leon tried to keep the balance, but the heavy vehicle skidded, went out of control, and plunged into a snowdrift. A sharp pain pierced Andrea's head, and she submerged into the darkness.

***

Andrea's head spun, making her dizzy and sick. She woke up in the morning in an unknown room. White walls, a beige carpet on the floor, heavy curtains to match, huge panoramic windows with a view to the volcano and the seafront.

She shot a glance at the mountain's summit and noticed how it had changed over the night. A huge mushroom-shaped cloud covered the top. The grey carpet of ashes ran down the slope.

A full English breakfast and a cup of freshly brewed coffee waited for her on a low bedside table, but the nausea was stronger than the smell of fried eggs and bacon. She felt a bit refreshed after having a shower, but the bruise on her temple still reminded her of last night's horror. She wondered what had happened to Leon when the door opened without a knock and a middle-aged woman dressed in black security uniform entered the room. Without further explanations, she demanded Andrea to follow her.

The house was enormous, built in a modernist style on the very edge of a cliff, with glass galleries connecting different parts of the building, a helipad, and an open-air heated pool.

Andrea tried to ask her minder about Leon and who were these people who chased them last night, but the woman struggled with English, and Andrea gave up finally.

When they arrived at the study, Leon had been waiting there for some time. Andrea rushed to him.

The next moment, the door opened, and a tall man in a long black military-style coat entered the room.

"Good morning, Miss Zissman, Mr Callais," he greeted Andrea and Leon in English. He smiled his crooked smile and took a seat behind a massive working desk. His accent sounded different from Icelandic. "My name is Frey Stefansson. I'm the Governor of this place," he continued.

"I demand to talk to somebody from the British Embassy," Leon barked. "You've taken two British citizens hostage. Your people chased, intimidated, and even tried to kill us yesterday. Do you understand the consequences?"

"I'm afraid the nearest British Embassy is in Reykjavik, Mr Callais."

"We require a call," Andrea said. "We're photographers, we came here to—"

"To spy on me and my people?" the Governor hissed.

"I don't understand what you are talking about. I don't understand what is going on." Leon's voice rose. "If we broke the local law or did something illegal, you would need to bring us to the police. Instead, you've locked us up here."

Looking at her friend, Andrea had to admit he looked even worse than she did. His hair, which he was always very particular about, was a complete mess. His clothes covered in dust, the dark circles around his eyes - everything pointed to a sleepless night.

"The nearest police station is in Akureyri. On an island with a population of two hundred citizens, we don't need a police station.

Everybody knows each other. We're a small peaceful community, living on this remote island, meaning no harm to anybody."

"What do you want from us?" Andrea asked, annoyed. She remembered the stories told by little Rufus, and now, looking at the Governor, she realised that this man could club to death not only baby-seals. She stared at his pale face and couldn't figure out how this handsome man could raise only disgust and anger in her soul. He was about her age. His deep brown eyes pierced her like the debris of volcanic rock.

"I need to know what you're doing here. Why are you spying on me and my people? I don't believe you came here to make a portrait of me or take an interview. You've intruded on private property. You've been told to leave, but you continued to violate the law instead."

"Listen, mister. We haven't done anything wrong, whereas you—"

"What you need to understand, Mr Callais, is that this land belongs to the colony." The Governor interrupted him. "Everything that is based, built, or lives here belongs to the colony as well. You've been told to leave, but you didn't listen."

"Why do we need to waste our time to prove our innocence? Who are you to accuse us?" Leon yelled.

Andrea wanted to get up and get out of the room when the double doors opened again, and two people, a man and a woman, entered the study.

The Governor nodded to his guards. "I do have evidence."

Andrea recognised the newcomers straight away. The man whom they'd met in the café for the first time, then near the warehouse, and the woman, his colleague.

The guards nodded to the Governor in greeting.

"Have you met these two people before?" he asked.

"Yes," the man replied first and told the whole story.

"We've also found this." His colleague took the drone out of her backpack and handed it to her boss.

"Hmm, it looks like—"

"It's a drone with a recording camera," the man said.

The Governor turned to Andrea and Leon. "So, what do you say now?"

Leon shrugged. "I don't know what these people are talking about. We've never seen them or this device before."

"Oh, so now you want to accuse my security guards of telling lies?" The Governor frowned. "Trust me, I've got enough witnesses." He nodded to the man.

The next moment, the barman appeared on the doorstep. He removed his hat, shuffling in an attempt to get rid of the snow on his boots and smiling almost apologetically to the Governor and his "guests".

The Governor greeted him and asked the same question he'd asked his security guards. The barman looked even more confused. He confirmed everything that had happened the morning before.

"Honestly, Governor, this is ridiculous." Andrea chuckled, trying to look as relaxed as possible. "Do you really think that we remember every barman we met, every café, every guest we talked to in Iceland?"

"Ah, you've probably got a slight case of amnesia when your snowmobile crashed, and you injured your head." The Governor grinned. "Of course, you can't remember every stranger, but I'm sure you're still able to remember a little orphan."

Andrea swallowed her shock back, but said nothing.

Following the Governor's gesture, one of the security guards came out of the study and returned with Rufus. His bright eyes were red from tears and, no doubt, a sleepless night in a cell.

The Governor knelt on one knee in front of him and said, "Good morning, Rufus. Tell me, please, have you seen these two people before?"

"Yes," the boy whispered, trying to avoid the Governor's eyes. "I met them yesterday on the beach."

"Did they ask you anything? Did they talk to you?"

"Yes, Mr Stefansson. They asked me about the school, about the tunnels, about you." He stammered, but the security guard pushed him slightly to make him talk.

"Please, carry on. Don't be afraid." The Governor smiled. "What else did they ask you about?"

"About the Temple of Aurora." He bowed his blond head really low, and tears filled his eyes.

The Governor turned back to Andrea and Leon. "What will you say to that?"

"You're a damn German bastard! That's enough. Let the boy go." Leon jumped from his chair.

"Oh, you're not going to surrender, Mr Callais, are you?" The Governor chuckled. "This is very unusual for the French, you know." He gestured to the two security guards, and the woman left the study, taking the barman and the boy with her.

Leon sat back in his chair. "This conversation makes no sense."

"You don't want to tell me the truth, so I need to learn everything myself. I'm sure I will. With your help or without it." He took Leon's laptop out of his desk drawer. "A password?"

Leon rose again and took one step closer to the Governor ready to claim his belongings back, but the security guard stood between them. The black metal of a gun shone under his unbuttoned jacket.

"Actually, I don't need a password. I'm sure my IT-guys will crack it in a few minutes, and I'll know everything I need to know about you." The Governor waved, then handed the laptop over to the guard. "Thank you, Einar. Let me know when the guys finish with it."

"Who gave you permission to touch our belongings? Who are we here? Your prisoners?" Andrea yelled.

"For the time being, you're my guests, Miss Zissman. I hope you'll enjoy my hospitality."

***

Frey stood in front of the window in his room and observed the sea. The black mass of the volcano produced thick smoke now, which could be seen from every corner of the island. The breeze blew vapours of sulphur.

He wondered whether they could see it from Akureyri, but the other, more important thoughts distracted him from his contemplation of the awakening giant. *These two intruders. How dangerous could they be for the colony and its mission?* He went to the bathroom and washed his face. It didn't help much. He looked in the mirror. His red eyes, his paler-than-normal face looked exhausted, his thick wavy hair looked dull. He felt even worse than he looked - dull and weak, thanks to hundreds of nights he spent without sleep. Insomnia and nightmares had been his best friends for years. He became immune to the high doses of alcohol and medication. Last night was no exception. He needed to swallow a quarter of a pack of pills to fall asleep. Literally, he put himself in a coma every night, without knowing whether he would be able to wake up or not, without thinking about it, without fear. These two made the matter even worse. He needed guidance now.

He came to a bookshelf and touched one of the books. The next moment, the wall moved, opening a passage, which slightly inclined and disappeared in the darkness of the rock. He took a step into this tunnel. The heavy secret door closed behind him without a sound.

He had been walking for about twenty minutes. The motion sensors reacted to the movements, so his way was well lit. The walls of the tunnel were in perfect condition, despite the fact that they were built many decades ago. He took a few turns. The crossroads didn't confuse him. He knew the route by heart as he followed it almost every day. Finally, the tunnel made the last turn, and an enormous door, about five metres high, appeared in front of him. It looked like a door to a bunker. He pressed his palm to a panel on the wall next to the door, and the next second, all of his body was scanned.

The heavy mass slid, opening the way to a spacious hall in the shape of a rotunda. All the walls were covered in some kind of ancient Germanic runes and fancy swastikas. The same complicated pattern of double and triple swastikas was on the dome-shaped ceiling and on the floor.

In the very centre of the rotunda, there was a pool, but instead of water, it was filled with the phosphorescent liquid. It changed its colour constantly – from bright green to deep purple, from yellow to dazzling white.

And there, in the centre of the pool, a body floated, wrapped in white sheets with plastic pipes connected to it. It was a man. He didn't look just old, he looked ancient - completely bald, with his long yellowish face, resembling a piece of ancient parchment all covered in deep wrinkles. The thin plastic pipes came out of his mouth and nose and disappeared into the bright liquid of the pool.

Frey came closer to the edge of the pool, and the man opened his colourless eyes. "Good morning, Father," he started in German, kneeling on one knee.

"Good morning, Frey," a low computer-generated voice replied, and the man bowed his bald head in greeting. "I expected you."

"My people caught two spies yesterday – a French journalist and his friend, a British woman."

"I'm aware of that," the man said. "I felt them coming."

"But how–"

"Don't underestimate the power of *Nothung*. I can see many things others can't. Remember?" The man paused. "These two are dangerous. They must never leave the island," he said finally. "We can't jeopardise our mission when it's so close to the final stage."

"I understand, Father, but…" Frey hesitated. "Wouldn't it be wiser to know who they are and who they really work for? If we get rid of them now without a proper investigation—"

"The nosey French moron and his Jewish half-breed mistress must die," the man barked.

"But—"

"What? I can see hesitation in your eyes, my dear. Where did this come from?" He squinted. His heavy, swollen eyelids without eyelashes didn't hide his look full of annoyance and sarcasm. "Oh, of course, you fancy this little Jew, don't you?" he continued, a shadow of a weak smile crossed his lips.

"Absolutely not."

"Please, don't tell me you're into this French guy. He-he!" Something that sounded like a crow's squawk reflected from the walls and the roof of the rotunda.

"Father! Please, stop it!"

"Okay, okay, don't take offence. I'm only joking," the man replied. "You're young and full of energy. You're forced to live here, on this remote island in the middle of nowhere, surrounded by rather rough men. You are bored. I understand that, but you can't put your own needs and whims above the mission. You can have some fun with the girl, but she and her friend must die before the end of the day."

Frey wanted to protest, but the man released a deep sigh, showing he had no intention of discussing this topic any longer. "I don't want these two to spoil everything. We've been waiting for so long. We can't fail now."

"The eruption is inevitable. Our station on the summit will be destroyed, but it doesn't matter. I can reassure you *Nothung* will be fully charged in less than twenty hours. Our people are on standby. Everybody is informed and ready."

The man sobbed. "I still can't believe it."

Frey saw all his body start to shiver in some kind of inaudible cry, but he had no tears to do it.

"I have been waiting for over seventy years and now only twenty hours separate me from seeing my Führer again," the man continued. "I can't afford to fail now."

"I won't let you down, Father." Frey rose from his knee. "You'll be proud of me. Our Führer will be proud of me."

"Go, Son, go. You know what to do." The man nodded.

"*Heil Hitler!*" Frey raised his arm in salute.

"*Heil Hitler!*" Otto von Koch replied, and his thin stick-like arm rose from the pool.

***

Andrea was alone in the room, circling in panic, seeing no way out. Leon's loud swearing still sounded like a bell in her ears. After their meeting with the Governor, they were separated. A female guard squeezed her arm and dragged her to her bedroom, while a guard, whom the Governor called Einar, pushed Leon somewhere downstairs, somewhere to the basement. A few hours had passed, and she still didn't know where he was.

It started to get darker. The long polar night was coming. The dark mass of Madgarjokull showed more and more attitude - the grey smoke turned into huge black exhausts. The building had been shaking over the past few hours. The raging ancient gods of this mystical land didn't bother Andrea at that moment, though. Her phone, Leon's laptop, their documents - everything had been taken from them.

To run? Where? To the frozen eternity of the glacier, to the raging Norwegian Sea? She had nobody in this world to look for her. *Leon, this trouble-maker, is the one who can help, but he himself is in trouble now.* Her thoughts were interrupted by the same guard who brought her here.

The woman carried a tray with plates and a plastic bag.

"Eat and get changed," she commanded.

A cold chill ran down Andrea's spine when she noticed a gun in the guard's holster.

The woman locked the door behind her back, and Andrea was left alone again. She glanced at the tray – baked fish with vegetables, crème-soup, even some fruits and cheeses. She chuckled. *At least, Mr Stefansson treats his prisoners well.* She hadn't eaten anything since breakfast, so the smell of freshly cooked salmon seduced her. An even bigger surprise had been waiting for her when she opened the plastic bag. *A bathrobe?* Andrea unfolded a white fluffy piece of clothing in hesitation. She had just put it on when the door opened again, as if she had been watched, and the same woman appeared at the door.

"Ready?" She frowned. "Let's go." She took Andrea's shoulder and pushed her to the door .

"Where are we going?"

The guard grinned. "To have a bath."

They went downstairs and entered a glass corridor, opening to a massive outdoor swimming pool. Light clouds of steam rose from the hot water. Despite the proximity of the awakening volcano, the night still felt frosty, but the underground hot springs provided not only the water for the pool, but the heat for the wooden floors. The guard left her alone at the pool. Oh, no! She was not alone.

"Ah, Andrea." The Governor appeared from under the water. "May I call you Andrea?" He moved closer to the edge. "I just thought you may like to experience bathing in the hot springs."

"I'm afraid, Mr Stefansson, I need to refuse your invitation. I haven't got a swimsuit with me." She tried to sound as confident as possible, though her knees were shaking.

"Don't worry. I haven't got my swimming shorts either." He continued to smile, biting his big lips. He rose slightly from the pool. His hand pulled the end of her gown's belt. The gown opened, showing her underwear. "Strip!" he barked, gritting his teeth.

There's no way out. Her whole body was shaking. *I will be raped and maybe even killed.*

"I said strip."

Her lingerie followed the robe.

The Governor arched his eyebrows. She could physically feel his sticky look.

He gestured for her to come into the water. "I'm very jealous of your French boyfriend."

"What have you done to Leon? Where is he?"

"Don't worry about him. If he and you behave well and answer all my questions, I won't harm him and maybe even let him join us."

She took a step into the pool. The water was warm, as if she had entered a hot bath. She could feel underwater streams massaging her skin.

He approached her. "Do you like your bath?"

"Mr Stefansson, you—"

He put his hand on her shoulder. "Please, call me Frey."

"Do you understand what you are doing?" She pushed his hands off. "You've kidnapped two British citizens. Your people tried to kill us. You continue to intimidate us, and now you're sexually harassing me. Do I need to continue the long list of your crimes? I'm afraid the whole night will not be enough to mention all of them."

"Please, darling," he said with a wry smile, "let me remind you something. It was you and your boyfriend who came here. Nobody invited you. You've been spying on us. I try to understand why you would do that. As I've already told you, we're a peaceful community. We've decided to stay here, away from civilization, away from all the troubles of this cruel and hypocritical world to live in dignity and harmony. We try to make this world and people better. We work as a charity. We even built an orphanage for poor souls. We're providing these kids with free education and looking after them. These children come from all over Europe, and we're ready to help. Whereas people like you, Andrea—"

"Damn! You know this is bullshit and a very good cover for your shady business."

"My business is not your concern."

"Let me and Leon go or—"

"Or what? Ah, you still don't get it, do you? Everybody on this island obeys me. Nobody will hear your complaints. The sweeter you are towards me, the better I'll treat you." His hand touched her neck. "Now, you tell me everything."

Andrea half-closed her eyes, preparing for the worst. An underground tremor made her lose her balance. She slipped on the pool floor, and a mini- tsunami created by the pool's waves buried her under the water for a few seconds. A moment later, two explosions ripped the air and… The whole world went silent.

"Oh, the old guy is showing his bad temper." Frey smiled, pulling Andrea from under the water and embracing her waist.

The earthquake continued for a couple of minutes. Andrea tried to break free from Frey's tight grip but failed. He was much taller and definitely stronger than her. He pushed her to the corner, gripping her neck.

The next moment, an underground vibration came back, this time even more powerful. Andrea pushed her abuser, and he disappeared in the waves.

The dark sky illuminated in all shades of red. A storm-like rumble penetrated the air.

"The volcano is starting to erupt. The island is dying." Andrea watched as the crater produced another black cloud of ashes. It spread rapidly and soon covered the whole sky. The heat wave punched her in the face, and the thick flakes covered everything around them.

"Oh, don't worry." Frey waved. "We're used to the tricks of this big guy."

Andrea noticed a special low table with a bottle of wine and a plate with fruits on the other side of the pool. A long, thin, fancy dagger for cutting fruits glittered in the dim reflection of the awakening volcano.

"Ah, of course." Frey followed her look. "Do you want some wine?" He swam closer to the table and picked up the dagger and a piece of mango.

"Some fruit?" he asked. "You see, I can be a thoughtful host. Just look at the beauty all around. Is it not cool to sit here, in an outdoor heated pool and enjoy the view of a raging volcano? Where else in Europe would you be able to see that? Enjoy yourself." He cut the mango and was going to give Andrea a half, but she didn't move, only

85

gritted her teeth and stared at him without a word. "Open your mouth." He moved closer again.

The thin blade of the dagger flashed in front of her face, and she felt its cold steel, touching her cheek. She opened her mouth slightly, and, the next second, felt the sour taste of mango.

"You're a real lady, so delicate, so soft." His fingers touched her lips. He was so close that she could feel his body was touching hers under the water. "You deserve a special, very sensitive approach."

His lips dived into hers. She tried to scream and pushed him away, but he jumped off. He had been staring at her for a few seconds, as if he would've seen a ghost. His face turned paler. His eyes expressed nothing but madness.

"Get out!" he yelled. "Put your clothes on and get out!"

She didn't need another invitation. She ran out of the pool, picked up her underwear, and disappeared behind the glass door.

***

Frey jumped out of the pool. He was out of breath, dizzy and sick. He'd had the visions before, but none of them were as powerful and realistic as that one.

The kiss... It felt so weird, so unnatural, as if he kissed a copy of himself. He closed his eyes and saw a mirror on fire. He stood in front of it, but couldn't see his reflection. It was Andrea in the mirror. The mirror exploded. Its razor-sharp debris went in all directions, piercing his face and naked body. He opened his eyes and shouted to Andrea in horror. Next, he fell on the slippery edge of the pool, grabbing his towel. His poor head was ready to explode. He had been lying without movement for a few minutes until the headache started to ease. He rose slowly, put his bathing robe on, and headed to his bedroom.

He lay down on the bed, closed his eyes, and tried to clear his mind. The floor and the furniture started to vibrate, receiving a new portion of the volcano's fury. This vibration ran through his body, and the visions returned with vengeance.

He was again a little boy in his parents' house. A glass door, leading to the garden, was opened. Climbing roses with fancy plump flowers, yellow and beige, hung down from frames, peeping into the opened windows. Their sweet and heavy smell filled the room. He heard his mother's voice. She called him in English. She called him his real name, but he was forced to forget it. He turned his head to the source of the voice in a desperate attempt to distinguish the name. He couldn't see his mother's face. There was a cradle in the corner of the room.

"Your mother and your sister are dead," the face of his stepfather morphed in front of him.

Fear and pain filled his soul. He started to cry and call for his real dad.

"Dad-d-dy, I-I-I-I… I want to see m-m-my daddy." He heard his voice.

There was another man in the room. He said something in an unknown language, but his stepfather only nodded and replied in English. "The kid is suffering from stammering, but we could treat it."

Treat it? The cold bare concrete walls, the dazzling white lights, the long metal table in the middle, wires connected to a machine, and a man in a white robe… pain, and more pain. He had already lost his voice, crying and calling for his parents.

"I've already told you, son. Your father killed your mother and your sister. He wanted to kill you as well. He was ill. His mind was clouded, and he went out of control. We needed to lock him up to save your life, but he killed himself." The face of his stepfather ebbed in again.

Then, there was "the treatment" with electrical shock again and again, and pain, and tears, and fear, and hours in the dark room.

The next vision morphed in his mind. The white sea of snow opened to him. He had never seen so much snow in his life. He could see the smiling eyes of his real father.

"Do you like it here?"

"Y-yes." He felt the speed, the icy prickles of snowflakes on his cheeks.

"Do you think Lulu the lion likes it here?"

"Y-yes, y-y-yes." He smiled, cuddling with his favourite toy.

"This is your new pupil." An unknown man, dressed in all black, was squeezing his hand and talking to a young lady. "His name is Frey Stefansson. Please, keep an eye on him. He needs a special approach."

"Get off my place, fucking half-breed."

The red pig-like eyes of Johan, his classmate, stared at him with contempt. Johan was much taller and stronger. He clenched his fists ready to attack. He was looking forward to any opportunity to mock Frey or beat him up.

"I'm not a half-breed." Despite the fact that he had no idea what "a half-breed" meant, Frey felt tears in his eyes. He attempted to get up from the snowdrift that Johan had pushed him into a moment before but struggled.

"Yes, you are." A blonde girl with two thin braids supported her brother. "Or even worse… a… a Jew!"

"That is even worse than a half-breed." Johan nodded.

"And your ugly lion? Is it also a Jew?" The girl chuckled. "How old are you? Only kids from Group A are playing with such toys."

"He's probably stolen it from them. That's what Jews normally do," Johan continued. "Mr Braum told us about them in the last lesson." He took one step closer and pulled the toy out of his hands.

"No, no, please, no." Frey shouted, jumping out of the snow, but Johan's punch knocked him down.

A few pupils laughed, watching the whole scene from the school's doorstep. The teacher had appeared as well, attracted by the shouts, but she did nothing, just stood there and stared at two kids fighting until they drew blood.

Frey stood in the centre of the classroom, all eyes were on him.

"Could you explain what happened? What's wrong with you?" the teacher questioned, grabbing his sleeve, digging her long red nails into his arm. "Maybe I need to report this case to repeat your treatment?"

"I promised Johan to pay him back one day, and I've done it." The ten-year old jerked back. "Today, I threw his pet guinea pig into a pan with boiling water. Tomorrow, he'll follow it."

He had promised to make his enemies suffer, and he kept his promise. Seven years later, he attacked Johan's sister in the school's changing room, then stabbed Johan to death in front of his classmates. He knew he would be beaten fearlessly for that. He knew he would be disciplined by his stepfather and his people, but it hadn't stopped him. He went too far that time. His stepfather could turn a blind eye on killing animals, Frey's constant fights with the classmates and quarrels with his teachers, but everything had its price. He was sent to a private college somewhere on the border between Austria and Germany.

He felt more freedom than ever. He plunged into madness of orgies, drugs, and alcohol. There was only one thing that entertained him more than drunken brawls and sex – violence. His stepfather's patience had become exhausted, and he ordered him to return to the island to continue his education remotely. There, completely cut off from the entire world, he felt free to do whatever he wanted to whomever he wanted. As soon as his stepfather was unable to continue his duties, he finally became the ruler of the place. In his traumatised mind, pleasure, power, pain, and horror went hand in hand to the point where he couldn't separate them from each other.

The loud knock at the door pulled him out of his reverie.

He tried to get up, but the headache still continued to chase him. "Come in," he shouted finally.

The door opened, and Einar appeared. "The password," he said and put Leon's laptop on one of the chairs. "The guys from IT have cracked it. You have access to all of his files now."

"Ah, thanks." Frey waved. "I'll have a look at it. You can go."

"The villagers, sir," Einar started, shifting on the doorstep, "they want to call for the rescue services. They want to evacuate as soon as possible. Panic is growing. We've already received a call from Akureyri. They feel tremors there. They want to—"

"No fucker is leaving the island without my permission," Frey barked. "What are they afraid of? Just a few tiny clouds? Tell them we're monitoring the volcano every hour. There is no danger."

"Will do." The guard nodded and left the room.

Frey switched the laptop on and stood in front of it in hesitation. The headache didn't allow him to focus. He opened one of the bedside table's drawers, took out a bottle of pills, and swallowed a handful of them. "Fucking journalist." He looked through the files. "Sniffing around, spying, digging shit out. What a bastard!"

One of the photos drew his attention.

The pills started to work, his head became heavy, the thoughts slowed down, but he fought against dizziness.

The photo or, better to say, a half of it depicted a tall man in his late thirties, dressed in a ski suit. Frey recognised these deep grey eyes, the smiling eyes of his father. The endless snowy landscape, the lonely mountain – the flat peak of Madgarjokull volcano – and him, a little boy, holding Lulu the lion.

He gasped for a deep breath, but struggled to fill in his lungs. He screamed in helpless grief and ran to his study. The reality turned into a nightmare, and his exhausted, sore brain was unable to separate them. Coming to one of the bookshelves, he moved it slightly. He pressed his finger to a special screen and pronounced a code, the metal door opened, revealing piles of documents and storage devices, but amongst all this the main thing – the secret that didn't allow him to sleep at night, the secret that chased him all these years, the secret that drove him mad.

A half of the photo – a slim young woman in a fur jacket, holding a year-old baby in a pink suit, the endless snowy landscape, the lonely mountain.

"Gabi, Gabi." He heard his mother's voice in his head. He was again a little boy in his parents' house. The garden, the roses in the window, the cradle in the corner...

"Gabi, Gabi," his mother's voice was calling him. "Come here. Don't disturb your sister."

Gabi. Gabriel. He continued to stare at the photo for a few seconds, then took Lulu the lion out of the safe.

The toy's colours faded away, one eye was missing, but for him this lion was the most precious thing in the world, the only thing that connected him to his past, to his real past, to his real self that he lost long ago. Lulu the lion – his one and only true friend, his only true love he had never betrayed, the only one who could calm him down and comfort him in his misery. Nobody could separate him from his Lulu, nobody could take him away, and nobody dared to mock Lulu.

He looked again at the photo and the toy. The tears flooded his eyes. He fell on the carpet, pressing his legs to his belly and cuddling with Lulu. His heart was pounding and echoing in his ears. His breath became short and quick, the cold disgusting sweat covered his face.

"Gabi, Gabi." The voice vibrated in his head.

The darkness surrounded him, and he plunged into a heavy, sticky, coma-like sleep.

***

Leon also experienced the Governor's "warm" hospitality. He was sitting on the ice-cold concrete floor in one of the rooms in the basement. The vibration was constant. A couple of pieces of plaster from the ceiling landed next to him. He stared at the white smoke of his breath without movement. His desire for a cigarette was unbearable, but even more unbearable was his feeling of despair. The uncertainty of his future didn't scare him much. All his thoughts turned to Andrea.

A heavy door opened, and the chief of security appeared. He stared at Leon for a second and… threw him a gun.

"I hope you can use it," he said in English. "Follow me."

Leon jumped, pointing the gun at the guard.

"Aha! I think you've forgotten something." The man pulled a magazine out of his pocket.

Leon put the gun down. "Why did you do that?"

"Please, we have no time for that." The guard handed him the magazine. "Do you want to live? If so, do what I say."

"Why should I trust you? A man who wanted to kill me and my friend."

"Do you have another choice? Besides," he paused. "If I'd wished to kill you, you would've been dead already."

Somebody's loud footsteps interrupted them. They could hear a few people running down the stairs, shouting and talking.

The man made a gesture to keep silent. "My name is Einar," he said when the sounds died away.

"I heard it. What is your real name?"

Einar sighed. "Mr Callais, how many times did my people ask you not to poke your curious nose in this business?"

"Ah, of course." Leon chuckled. "*Shalom*, Agent Chaim! Or maybe Shlomo? Last time I talked to your colleagues, they tried to intimidate me, requesting to stop my independent investigation immediately. They were extremely persistent, you know. The Mossad's methods aren't any better than the Governor's—"

"I can't believe how naive you are." Einar shook his head. "You put not only your useless life in danger, but also the life of the poor woman."

"Her real name is Andrea Owen. She needs to know the truth about her father. She deserves to know what happened to her family. Whereas you and your people… You do everything to stop her. The deposit box in London? What was in it?"

Einar's pale eyes flashed in the dim artificial light of the basement, but he replied nothing.

"Why do you want to help us?" Leon repeated. "If we're in your way, why not just allow the Governor to get rid of us and continue your operation?"

"Because I'm not like the Governor." Einar gritted his teeth. "My task is to find *Standartenführer* Otto von Koch and bring him to justice. This man must be judged for all his crimes against humanity and, above all, against the Jews. He must be punished for the inhuman experiments he had been leading during the construction of *Nothung*, using us like a material to see how the power of the device influenced a human's body."

"What?" Leon chuckled. "Do you hear yourself? At the end of the war, Koch was in his early thirties. Now, he must be over one-hundred-year—"

"The power of *Nothung* is keeping him alive," Einar continued. "Thousands of Jews had been killed during the experiments Koch's team of doctors and scientists were conducting in order to understand how the Jews could be cleansed from their 'Jewishness'. He believed that they could be treated for it like for an illness."

"What a lot of bullshit!"

Einar grimaced. "Oh thank you, Captain Obvious."

"*Nothung*? What about it?"

"They keep it underground. All I saw was a tunnel that went to the Temple of Aurora. I'm sure the device is there. It produces such a powerful magnetic pulse that it disables all electronics within a few metre radius. The fields disabled the micro-camera that I had attached to Frey's jacket…" He stammered. "I've spent several years studying German and Icelandic, reading, researching, and preparing myself for this mission. Trust me, Frey is the most dangerous, suspicious, and cruel psychopath I've ever met. His brain is completely fucked up, but he's smart enough to keep all the device's codes in his memory. Only he and Koch know how to program and operate *Nothung*. It took me about a year to make Frey trust me, to become his best mate, his companion in the endless disgusting 'entertainments' and now—"

Leon snorted. "Please, don't try to play Mr Nice Guy now. The Mossad is for the Mossad only."

"You still don't understand how dangerous *Nothung* is, do you?" Einar squinted. "There are only a couple of hours left till it will be fully charged. If Koch's calculations are correct, the power of *Nothung* will be enough to generate the electromagnetic pulses of such intensity that they could destroy every single navigation system on the planet, including missile launching systems and satellites. While the world's leaders will be blaming each other in this chaos, panicking, and proclaiming war, *Nothung* will open the portal."

"The portal? Is it real?"

"It looks like that. The portal will bring back the Führer and all the SS leaders who went with him in 1945. These seventy years will have passed like one second for them. When they arrive, Frey and Koch will raise their army of followers all over the world. These people have money, power, and weapons. Frey has spent years building his personal Reich. From Germany, Austria, and Norway to Argentina and Chile – there are colonies like 'Aurora' everywhere. The colonists and their followers swore loyalty to the Führer and to Frey, of course. This loyalty is built on money, fear, hatred, but most of all, on strong faith in the Leader. Whether the Führer will arrive or not, Frey is already their Leader."

"He's a psychopath. Why would all these people follow him?"

"The Nazi gold had brought them together. Besides, Frey's preaching is popular nowadays in Europe and the rest of the world." Einar shrugged. "Western civilization is ill. Frey thinks he's found a cure."

"Wait a minute." Leon squinted. "That's why you're here – to kill two birds with one stone."

"What are you talking about?"

"Oh, come on. To catch *Standartenführer* is only a part of your task, but to turn Frey and *Nothung* against the old enemies of Israel – that is a real business. In a few minutes, the power of *Nothung* could vaporise half of the Middle East and—"

"I thought you were a curious troll, hungry for sensational shit. No. You're just a complete moron," Einar snapped. "This island is dying. The volcano has started to erupt. The villagers are in a panic, but Frey and his people pay no attention. His helicopter is ready and even a mini-sub in one of the underground grottos is put on standby. I'm going now to save your girl and as many villagers as I can. If you're so bloody delicate, you can—"

"I'm going with you. What about the cameras?" Leon pointed to the dark lump on the ceiling.

"Don't worry. I've taken care of that."

***

The door swung open, and Frey appeared on the doorstep with Leon's laptop in his hands.

Oh, no! Andrea moved in the far corner of the bedroom. *No escape from the psychopath this time.* "Why are you here? To torture me again? To finish what you have started in the pool?" she yelled.

"Where did you get this?" He opened the laptop and nodded at the picture of her father and little brother. His eyes looked swollen, his voice sounded lower.

Andrea gritted her teeth. "This is a photo of my father, Dr George Christopher Owen, and my older brother Gabriel Owen. The only photo of them I have." She raised her head. "And I am Andrea Owen. I'm here to find the truth about their death."

An oppressive pause filled in the room. Only the loud rumble and noises of the explosions from the volcano interrupted it.

Frey mumbled something, his hands were shaking. "No. No, it can't be true." He backed away to the door.

She shrugged. "Yes, it is. That's why Leon and I are here."

Without saying a word, he took half of an old photo out of his pocket, and Andrea gasped in shock, covering her mouth with her hand.

The photo depicted a slim young woman in a fur jacket, holding a year-old baby in a pink suit, the endless snowy landscape, the lonely mountain…

Andrea recognised her mother and herself. "What does it mean?"

"And this is Lulu the lion." Frey took the cuddly toy out of another pocket.

Andrea sunk into her bed. "Did you know my father and brother?" She swallowed her upcoming tears back. "No. It can't be right. You were far too young to… God!" Her head spun. "You're about the same age as Gabriel would've been… Oh, no!" The thought was so terrifying, so bizarre to say it out loud. "You're not… You can't be."

He leaned against the wall, his arms dropped, and the laptop hit the floor. "I didn't know. I'm sorry, so sorry," he repeated it again and again. "I've been told my father killed my mother and wanted to kill me."

"Our mother spent all her life in a special care home, forced into silence until her death, too scared to speak about what had happened here." Andrea shook her head. "She died a few weeks ago. My grandma raised me alone. She never told me a thing about my father and you." She told him the rest of the story.

He didn't interrupt. "My stepfather lied to me, lied all my life. He wanted me to kill you and the journalist. He wanted me to—" His fists clenched, and he stopped.

Andrea rose from the bed and came closer. He studied his face. His dark brown eyes with long lashes, his wavy, black hair, his pale face. He was the boy from her dreams, the little astronaut in the photo.

"And your stepfather's name was,' she paused for a second. "Otto von Koch, I guess."

"And it still is. The monster is still alive, still poisoning me and everybody else with his lies." He took her hand in his. "But I'll squeeze the truth out of him. I'll make him suffer for everything he's done to me, you, and our family."

"Koch is still alive?" Andrea shook her head. "How is it possible?"

"Because of *Nothung*. Ah, it's a long story." He waved. "I need to know the whole truth. I need…" He squeezed his temples, then grabbed her hand again. His eyes pleaded. "I know you'll never forgive me or forget what happens to you here, but at least I hope you won't hate me." With that said, he opened the door.

"Where're you going?" Andrea shouted. "Locking me up again?"

"I'm going to find out the truth, and you... You'll be safe here." He paused at the door, staring at her. "I'll come back for you. Nothing will separate us anymore. I promise."

"Wait, please. Killing Koch won't change anything." She squeezed his shoulder. "It won't bring our father back. Koch must face trial for all his crimes. *Nothung* must be stopped. Justice must rule, not revenge."

A crook smile distorted his face. "Don't you think you've been waiting for justice for far too long?"

Andrea wanted to object, but the door closed behind him. She took a seat back on the bed in silence. Tears were streaming down her cheeks. She screamed, but only the low rumble of the volcano answered her.

***

"It was you who killed my father, who separated me from my family, who silenced my mother forever." Frey kneeled at the edge of the pool in the Temple of Aurora. His hands squeezed Koch's neck.

"And now you wanted me to rape and kill my sister!" he shouted the last words, tears filling his eyes. "What a monster you are!"

The old man coughed. "Who do you believe? This French clown? Your father worked for us, that's true. The power of the lights possessed his mind. He was going to kill everybody, to destroy *Nothung*, to put our mission at risk. I couldn't allow it to happen. I wanted to protect you. I wanted to lock him up, but he committed suicide. You know that."

"Protect me? Or *Nothung* and yourself? Your people tortured me, beated me up, abused me. Is that what you call 'protection'?"

"You still don't understand," Koch hissed. "You were a weak, ill child with learning and speech issues. You had no future, but now… look at you. You're the Leader. Hundreds of thousands will follow you. You will rule this world."

"I'm a murderer, a monster. I'm no better than you," Frey murmured, loosening his grip and stepping away from the edge of the pool.

"Listen to me, Frey," Koch whispered, "our dearest Führer isn't young and he's very ill. Soon after his arrival, he will need to appoint his successor. You, my son, the best possible candidate for that. You will become the next Leader."

"I'm the Leader of the New Reich? I'm the Führer's successor?" Frey laughed. "I think your Führer will be surprised, knowing that his successor is actually a Jew."

"Bullshit!" The old man's eyes fired daggers. "I respect my Führer, but he made a huge mistake, exterminating all Jews instead of making a deal with them. He listened to all the fancy crap that the idiots like Himmler, Eichmann, and others were spreading. All their fairy tales about Aryans, German knights, and Valkyries are nothing but bollocks. You, Frey... You're the best evidence of my theory."

"Your theory?"

"I'm going to prove to my Führer that anybody can build his personal Reich." He clung to the edge of the pool. "Even such a weak Jewish boy like you. You're my best creation, Frey. You're my most successful evidence of—"

"Evidence," Frey repeated. The vision of the mirror came back to him. The debris pierced his body again, then...

"Gabi, Gabi..." His mother's voice sounded like a lullaby.

He saw the room with opened windows, his mother's smiling face, blooming roses, and a cradle in the corner.

"Your experiment has failed. Say hello to your Führer. I hope you'll meet him in hell!" he shouted these last words in Koch's face, squeezing his shoulder, pulling a plastic tube out of his mouth, and pushing him back into the pool.

The thin body plunged into the thick waves. The next moment, his head rose above the pool's edge to make his last agonising gasp and disappeared in the phosphorescent liquid.

***

"Thank God, you're alive!" Andrea's eyes were burning with tears, her knees bent, and she almost fell into Leon's open arms.

"Are you alright? What has he done to you?" he whispered in her ear, stroking her hair.

"Nothing. I'm fine, fine. I need to tell you something."

"I totally understand your excitement, guys, but we haven't got time for that," Einar's low voice sounded from the doorstep.

Andrea took a couple of steps away in the far corner of the room.

Leon made a warning gesture. "Don't worry, he's an agent."

"An agent?"

"He's with us. He freed me from my cell," Leon continued. "I'll tell you the whole story later."

"Hurry up!" Einar interrupted him. "We need to get out of here before it's too late."

As proof of his words, the floor vibrated vigorously, and they had to grab pieces of furniture to keep their balance. The vibration turned into waves. Pieces of plaster showered down on them from the ceiling. A heavy mirror fell from a wall spreading its sharp debris all over the room. A thin web of cracks appeared in the triple-glazed panoramic windows, bombarded by the hail of pumice the size of an egg.

"Damn!" Einar grabbed the door's handle. "Hurry! We need to get to the tunnel. This is the shortest way to the village."

They ran out of the room to a pitch-black empty corridor.

"Everybody has already left the building." Einar turned to the couple.

They went downstairs, trying to be as quiet as possible with their guns ready.

The building continued to shake. All the windows had been smashed, and pieces of the broken furniture were strewn everywhere. The thick layer of pumice covered the floor, reaching their ankles.

Einar pointed to one of the rooms, where the door was slightly open. "Here." He entered the room first, checking every corner, and waved for them to follow him. "This is one of the Governor's private rooms," he explained. "The tunnel leads from here to every corner of the island. You need the one that goes to the village."

"What about you?" Leon asked.

"I need the one that leads to the Temple of Aurora. I must stop *Nothung*. I must find Otto von Koch."

"But it means that—" Leon started, but Andrea interrupted him.

"Wait. I need to tell you that I've found my brother," she shouted.

Leon turned to her. "Really? How? Where's he?"

"It's Frey." She exhaled.

"What? Is it true?" Leon turned from her to Einar and back. "And you knew, didn't you?" He pointed his gun at Einar's head. "You knew everything from the very beginning. The documents from the deposit box you've stolen? It was all there. Still, you wanted to kill us, so we wouldn't spoil your mission."

Einar bowed his head. "That's not true."

"So tell me the truth then." Andrea took a step closer. "Whoever you are – a security guard, a Nazi or a secret agent, an angel or a demon... Please, tell me the truth."

"Right." He sighed. "We haven't got much time, though."

Andrea nodded to Leon, and he put the gun down.

"The name of the SS-officer, who stood in charge of the project *Nothung*, disappeared from all radars in 1945 when the U-boat U-977 made her last trip from Norway to Midgardur Island. He emerged from the past under a fake name in 1985 when he was accused of some shady tax fraud. Nothing to do with your father's murder."

"How did Koch know my father? Why did he want to kill him? My father came to Iceland to work on his research."

"Soon after the expedition arrived in Iceland, the university ran out of money and decided to stop funding the project. Your father believed in his theory so much that he refused to end the research and go back to England. Instead, he continued on his own. Such a risky enterprise required lots of effort and money. The second one was melting rapidly. Then, Otto von Koch or Richard Adler, as he was known here, appeared and offered Dr Owen not only full funding for his project, but also provided the most luxurious accommodation for him and his family in Akureyri, a private jet to travel, and many, many other perks, which the scientist couldn't even dream of while working at his university. Your adventurous mother couldn't stay long without her husband and decided to visit him in Akureyri."

"My father wouldn't have worked for the Nazis, if—"

Einar continued, "According to his contract, Richard Adler represented some German company that was looking for a new alternative source of cheap energy. When Dr Owen knew the truth, it was too late. Koch didn't want to let your father go, but he started to threaten him that he was going to tell the press about Koch's shady business, and…" Einar bowed his head and squeezed Andrea's hands. "These people, Andrea, nothing can stop them, only death."

"How did my mother survive? How did she manage to save me?"

"I don't know. Probably, somebody helped your mother and she escaped, saving you, but she failed to save your brother. It seems like Koch had no intention to kill him, but to bring him up in the Nazi tradition." He embraced her shoulders and whispered in her ear, "I'm sorry, girl. There is nothing left of your brother anymore."

A pause as heavy and cold as a glacier filled up the room.

"You said that the authorities found out about Koch's shady business." Leon broke the silence. "Why didn't they continue the investigation? Why the British police wasn't involved? Why is Koch still here?"

"According to the disclosed files of this case, Koch had been taken to jail, but died a few weeks after his arrest, suffering from a heart attack."

Leon frowned. "Wait a minute. Are you saying that our *Standartenführer* faked his death to escape justice?"

"The case was closed suspiciously quickly. The colony was left without a leader for a while. About six months later, Mr Abel Weiss, a seventy-something-year-old German entrepreneur arrived. The nature of his business, his income, and his past were just as mysterious as Mr Weiss' identity. Being a German citizen, he couldn't be elected as a Governor. However, in the next few years, he bought almost the whole of Midgardur Island. He also adopted a child, a four-year-old Icelandic orphan, Frey Stefansson.

"Frey suffered from speech difficulties, dyslexia, and some other health issues, just as Gabriel Owen did. Frey was raised in the atmosphere of terror, threat, fear, torture, and even murder. Almost three decades later, he became the dignified heir of Otto von Koch."

A new portion of underground tremors distracted Einar's story. The floor started to shake again. The cracks went through the ceiling and the walls. One of the windows exploded. A blast of icy wind hit the heavy air of the room. A few low bangs tore the night up, and the sky coloured in all shades of red.

"We need to speed up." Einar hurried up but struggled to keep his balance.

"I need to find my brother," Andrea said. "We can't leave him here."

"Girl, you're even crazier than your brother," Einar shouted in her ear. "Richard Adler, Abel Weiss, Otto von Koch. This man of many names allowed your brother to live for two reasons only – to prove his insane theory and to create a monster. He brought him up as a monster. He treated him as a monster. So your brother became a monster. Gabriel Owen died many years ago when Frey Stefansson was born. He doesn't even deserve to leave the island. Don't you understand?"

"Don't you understand that he's still my brother?" Andrea screamed. "He will face trial for his crimes, but it should be a fair trial. If we leave him here to die, are we any better than Koch? I've only just found my brother, resurrected him from the dead. I don't want to lose him again."

Einar didn't listen to her last words. He reached to the bookshelf and touched one of the books. The tunnel's door moved aside, opening the dark throat of the underground maze. The next moment, a heavy ceramic vase crashed on the back of the agent's head.

"Sorry, buddy," Leon said, the rest of the vase in his hand. "From now on, we don't really need your help."

"God! You've killed him." Andrea stood in front of Einar's body in shock.

"No. He'll wake up in half an hour with a tiny bruise on his head. Don't worry about him." He took a seat next to her and embraced her shoulders. "My brain wants to follow him and his logic, but my heart tells me to follow you. We need to find your brother and leave the island together. Let's go."

"No, I need to do it myself. You need to go."

"I won't leave you alone here."

"I don't think we require your services, Mr Callais." Frey appeared from the darkness of the tunnel. His gun pointed at Leon's head.

Andrea ran to him. "Brother, please!"

"Drop your weapon and turn around." Frey didn't listen to her.

Leon put his gun on the floor, but didn't say a word.

"Let's go." Frey grabbed Andrea's hand and pulled her to the tunnel. "We need to get out of here. I promised not to leave you again. I'm going to keep my promise."

***

"Where're you taking me? To your helicopter? What about the villagers? There're kids there. Even if rescue services arrive, they won't have enough time to help everybody. They need our help." Out of breath, Andrea was pushed and dragged deeper and deeper into the dark throat of the tunnel.

The floor and the walls were covered in cracks. Pieces of plaster and dust showered down on them from all directions. One of the light fittings fell, hitting Andrea's head. "Ouch!"

Her brother was oblivious to everything that was going on around him, though.

"Stop it! I'm hurt." Andrea jerked his sleeve, showing him her palm covered in blood from the wound on her head.

"Not far now, not far at all."

They turned around a corner, and an intensive white light made Andrea blind for a few seconds.

"This is it." He pointed to the source of the light. "We are going to a new, better world, the world that will belong to us. The world where there are no wars, no evil, no violence, the world where we will be worshipped as gods, the world where we can live in peace."

She looked at his face. His dark eyes shone in fever, his hair was in a mess, his arms and shoulders were covered in dust.

"Gabriel, you're delirious. You're ill, you need help." She put her hand on his forehead.

"Gabriel? You called me Gabriel. That means that you can forgive me." He smiled his insane smile. "I've been used. You know that." He stammered, and she saw tears, shining in his eyes. He sat on the concrete floor, dropping his gun and pulled her down.

"I know. We were both victims," she said. She couldn't figure out the sudden change in his mood. She saw him in shock a couple of hours ago, but now, he turned into an annoyed, dangerous villain again. *He's unstable. He doesn't understand what he's doing.*

"Don't worry. I've taken my revenge for both of us."

She stared at him. "What do you mean?"

"Otto von Koch is dead," he continued, "I killed him and reprogrammed *Nothung*. The Führer and his followers will never come back. They're stuck hundreds of thousands of worlds away. But we… Using the power of the device, we can go to a better place than this cruel, evil, backward world."

"What are you talking about?"

He gestured to the source of the light. "Look."

She turned around and shielded her eyes from the dazzling light. Now, she could distinguish that they sat on the floor of a round, rotunda-like room. A heavy, thick metal door was opened wide. She noticed a pattern of double and triple swastikas on the dome-shaped ceiling and on the floor.

In the centre of the room, some kind of a platform arose from a round pool filled with the phosphorescent liquid. The platform was surrounded by curved beams that dazzled Andrea with their white light. The phosphorescent waters of the pool moved, creating a weird pattern of frozen waves.

"This is *Nothung*," he said with pride. "It will take us to the other side."

"The other side of what?"

"This world is dying, so let it die. People are killing each other for nothing, so let them be killed. Trust me, Andrea, on the other side, where the skies are dark blue, two suns are always in the sky, the golden spires of temples rise above the skyline, where there is no sorrow, no grief, no death, no pain, we will become the new gods of this land."

"How do you know? How can you be so sure that this 'new world' even exists?"

"I saw it in my visions many times. I've been there."

"Oh, Gabi..." She looked into his eyes, but saw nothing apart from madness. "It's just a product of your exhausted mind. You need to go with me. You need help."

"To go with you? With these people? This French moron and this traitor, Einar?" He pushed her back. "They want me dead."

"No. We'll return home to England. You'll have a fair trial. I will be with you, I promise. You need to relax, to free your mind from everything. I know some good doctors who will help you. You'll feel better. I'll visit you every day. You'll start a new life. We both will."

He squeezed her shoulders. "Do you promise? Do you promise not to leave me?"

She embraced him and cuddled, as if he had become her older brother again.

"Hands up! Leave her alone!" Leon and Einar's voices echoed all around the rotunda.

"Please, don't shoot!" Andrea screamed.

"Get out of the way." Leon circled them. "This man is dangerous."

"This man is under arrest," Einar barked.

"No, no," she mumbled. "He's crying, he's scared, he's ill. Don't you see? Let me deal with him. Let me do it alone. He won't listen to anybody apart from me. There's no need for violence."

The next second, the walls, the floor, and the ceiling - everything started not just to vibrate, but to jerk in some unpredictable rhythm. A huge crack ran from the floor to the ceiling. The gap grew wider. The waves in the pool stopped. The curved beams of *Nothung* began to spin around the platform.

"Quick, Andrea, quick!" Gabriel rose from the floor, picked up his gun, and pulled Andrea closer to the pool.

"Don't move!" Einar shouted.

A shot reflected from the rotunda's walls. Andrea screamed. Einar swore when he realised that he had missed.

"Ouch!" A piece of a metal reinforcement bar pierced Leon's shoulder.

Gabriel shot, trying to stop Einar, but the floor waved and made him miss.

The crack ran straight under the pool, the dazzling light of the beams became dim blue. One of the beams extinguished completely, and the next second, it fell, burying everything under its colossal weight.

The last thing Andrea saw was her brother, who pushed her away, and a thick cloud of suffocating grey dust filled up the room.

He was lying on the floor motionless. The lower half of his body was buried under the debris of the beam. He turned his dusty face to her. "Andrea." He stretched his hands out in the last weak attempt to be rescued.

"Gabriel, no! Oh, no!" She rushed to him, trying to free him from his trap, but he only groaned.

A tiny stain of dark blood appeared on his pale lips. "I'm so sorry for everything I've done," he whispered.

She kept on pulling him.

"Sorry, girl, but you need to leave him."

She felt Einar's heavy palm on her shoulder.

"His legs and internal organs are squashed," he continued. "Even if we manage to move this debris—"

"We can't just leave him here."

"Einar is right." Gabriel opened his eyes. "Just tell me that you forgive me, that you'll never forget me, and go."

"I'm not leaving without him. I'm not leaving," she repeated again and again.

"Sorry, but we have no time for sentiments."

These were the last words Andrea heard. With the agility of a cat, Einar grabbed her neck and pressed a tiny vein under her chin. And the world around her went dark.

***

She spent a couple of days in the hospital in Akureyri together with some other villagers, injured during the eruption. Leon visited her every day. He didn't want to return home alone. She didn't talk to him. She didn't want to see him. She just turned her back to him and stared into space every time he entered the ward.

Once, she met little Rufus in the reception area. Despite his broken arm and a couple of bruises, he looked happy and excited. He told her he had found a new home. A family from Reykjavik was ready to adopt him.

"They're kind people, they really like me." He beamed. "I won't need to do all the hard work anymore. I'll even have my own room and lots of toys. They promised to buy me a puppy for Christmas if I do well in school."

She only smiled in reply. She wanted to ask him so many questions, but the words just stuck in her mouth. A nurse called him. Giving Andrea a peck in the cheek and a promise to meet her again, Rufus disappeared in one of the hospital's corridors.

A few days later, she and Leon took a short flight to Reykjavik, then a long one back to London.

Leon tried to start a conversation a couple of times, tried to take her hand, but every time faced the cold thick wall of her contempt. She locked herself inside a castle of silence like her mother did many years ago.

He gave her a shy kiss on the cheek at the airport and wished she would change her mind, but she didn't answer again.

***

A long dark month had passed since Andrea left the doomed island. Dozens of missed calls, unread emails and texts, and endless deleted voice messages nagged at her. Her whole life turned into one long, sticky, nightmarish existence. Her best friends tried to support her, advised to visit a counsellor, but it made her anxiety grow even more. Despite her wish, she couldn't stop thinking about Leon. After all, he was the one who discovered the truth for her.

Would have I been happier, refusing Leon's offer to go to Iceland? This thought kept torturing her exhausted mind. *The truth. The truth is always painful, but was I ready to endure so much pain? No. I wasn't ready for the truth. Would I ever be? No, but after all, it isn't Leon's fault. I asked him to help me. He has nothing to do with my family and its problems, and now, he's the one whom I make suffer. Yet, he still wants to be here for me.*

After a few days of struggle, she finally decided to talk to him. With no particular plans for Christmas evening, she gambled to invite him over.

***

"Merry Christmas," Leon greeted her with a shy smile, entering the house and shifting on the doorstep.

"Merry Christmas!" Andrea smiled in reply. "I'm really happy you've managed to come. I wasn't sure. I thought you would rather spend Christmas with your family or wouldn't celebrate at all."

"Ah." He waved. "I went there for a couple of hours. The place was full of my stepbrothers' kids, their dogs, their friends, their wives, their wives' relatives. I just gave everybody their gifts and left that madhouse as soon as possible."

"You're such a family person." Andrea chuckled. "How is your shoulder, by the way?"

"Ah, just a scratch left."

They went to the dining room. Christmas dinner was ready.

"We're not waiting for anybody else," she said. "So help yourself."

"I brought gifts for you. The gifts go first." He rose from the table and went back to the living room where he had left all his bags.

"Thank you, but this can wait."

His face became serious. "Others can, but this one definitely can't." He handed her one of the two paper bags he had brought with him. "I received it from Israel a few weeks ago."

She opened the bag and couldn't believe her eyes. An old, faded photo in a thin wooden frame – her father, her mother, Gabriel, and herself – all together in the background of Madgarjokull volcano.

"I glued the two parts together and put it in the frame," Leon said. "Here is something else." He pulled out a large plain envelope. "The documents that Einar's people removed from the deposit box. Your parents' marriage certificate, Gabriel's birth certificate, and so on. Also, I've found this in the parcel."

It was Lulu. The lion survived.

Andrea's eyes were burning with tears, Leon embraced her shoulders. "There was no return address on the parcel," he continued. "I'm sure it was from him."

"Agent Einar or whatever his real name is..." She raised her eyes to him. "Why didn't he send it directly to me? I'm pretty sure it wouldn't be a big deal for him to find my address."

"Maybe he wanted me to deliver it to you." Leon winked. "He saw your condition. He wanted you to recover. He isn't a bad person. He's just a man who serves his country. He won't stop. He will be hunting people like Otto von Koch until he finds them, finds them all. By the way, it was he who rescued Rufus from the collapsing house."

"What happened to Koch's people?"

"Most of them have been arrested. They're awaiting trial now. It looks like the villagers started to talk, but there are others. Agent Einar still has lots of work to do."

"I'm not judging him or you." She nodded and took a seat on the coach.

"When I saw Gabriel was taking you away, I knew he wanted to escape, but I didn't know what he was going to do to you. You were my priority. That's why I helped Einar."

"I know." She bowed her head. "I thought about it again and again. Call me a Nazi sympathiser, call me a hypocrite, call me insane, call me whatever you want to call me, but I've forgiven my brother, forgiven him for everything. Now, you can leave me and go. I won't be offended." She clutched the toy lion.

"You've done everything right." He looked directly into her eyes. "As for me, I'll never judge you, and... I'm not leaving you."

She snuggled closer to him and smiled. Her tears dried up. "I've lost my brother, but I've found you."

He frowned. "Oh, I thought I might've done better."

"Better?"

"Better than a brother, you know."

She chuckled. "I've already told you I don't date an ashtray."

"I haven't been smoking for three days."

"I appreciate your effort, but I don't need more sacrifices. That's why I've also bought you a gift." She went to another room and appeared with a small box wrapped in the colourful paper.

"That's so nice of you," Leon muttered, unwrapping the gift. "Of course, an electronic cigarette."

"No more ash, no more smell, no more stubs, no more—"

"No more excuses for saying 'no'." He pulled her closer and didn't let her finish.

It was a proper French kiss, hot, passionate, and seductive, but Leon managed to make it soft, sweet, and tender.

"This is the best Christmas gift I've ever had," he whispered.

Valeriya Salt is a multi-genre author from the United Kingdom. She studied history and earned her Master's degree in Art Expertise at St. Petersburg University of Culture and Arts. Born in Belarus, she'd lived for many years in different corners of Eastern Europe before settling down in the north of England. Her short stories, essays, and reviews have appeared in anthologies and magazines, including *The Copperfield Review, Bewildering Stories, Strange Fiction 'Zine SF&F, The Pine Cone Review*, etc., and won a Honourable Mention in the Writers of the Future contest. Her sci-fi thriller novel *Dive Beyond Eternity* is out in 2023 by Northodox Press (UK).

Follow Valeriya on:

Twitter: @LSalt1

Facebook: www.facebook.com/saltandnovels

Printed in Great Britain
by Amazon